Rewrite The Stars

Sarah Emambocus

Published by Sarah Emambocus, 2022.

REWRITE THE STARS

First edition. May 10, 2022.

Copyright © 2022 Sarah Emambocus.

ISBN: 979-8201071189

Written by Sarah Emambocus.

Table of Contents

Chapter 1

The story begins in London where a young woman is shopping when someone calls her name, *"Destiny"*. Destiny turns around and sees it is her best friend, Jennifer. Jennifer hugs her and says, *"let's finish shopping and grab a coffee ok!"*. After they have done shopping, they sit in a posh café as Jennifer asks, *"where have you been? I haven't seen you in ages!"*. Destiny replies *"that's Maxwell for you!"*. Jennifer says, *"I can't believe that you are still together with him."* Destiny drinks her coffee as she chats with Jennifer however her phone rings and she sees Maxwell calling her. Destiny answers as Maxwell says, *"it has been over two hours since you left the house what's taking so long?"*. Destiny says, *"I am coming back soon."*

Jennifer says, *"Destiny you need to divorce Maxwell."* Destiny says, *"I don't want Molly to suffer the first few years of her life."* Jennifer says, *"you both can come live with me."* Destiny says,*" I will keep in contact with you"*. Jennifer and Destiny exchange numbers as she leaves. She gets home as she finds Molly crying as Maxwell is drunk off his head as Destiny says angrily, *"Max what the hell?"*. Destiny comforts Molly and prepares her some food. Later that evening as Destiny puts Molly to bed; when Destiny comes downstairs she sees her husband. Maxwell turns to Destiny and says, *"I am off to the pub"*. Destiny asks, *"do you have to go?"*. Maxwell replies coldly, *"you don't expect me to wait around in this dump"*. As he left Destiny cleans up the empty glass bottles as she sits down. Destiny calls Jennifer and says, *"please come and pick me and Molly up!"*.

Jennifer comes in her car as Destiny packs everything and leaves her wedding ring on the table as she and Molly drive away with Jennifer. Jennifer brings her to her house which is a few miles away; as Destiny places Molly on the couch as Jennifer says, *"let me get you a glass of juice."* Destiny cries as Jennifer says, *"I am here for you and Molly."* Destiny drink the juice as she soon feels tired as Jennifer says, *"you can sleep in my room."* Destiny has a nightmare that Maxwell comes in drunk and tries to take her back. The next morning, she sees 100 missed calls from Maxwell including 20 messages and 80 voicemails. Destiny comes down as Jennifer cooks breakfast. Jennifer says, *"I am going to manage your divorce, you just focus on getting a job."* Molly says, *"mommy?".* Destiny asks, *"do you have some cereal Jen?".* Jennifer replies, *"I will prepare it."*

Destiny drops Molly to school as Maxwell sees her and comes to her. Destiny says *"Maxwell."* Maxwell says angrily, *"you thought you could leave me?".* Destiny says *"enough is enough! I can't stay with you anymore. you neglect Molly and you are an alcoholic."* Maxwell grabs her hand as someone comes and pushes him off. Destiny turns and is shocked to see who it is. The guy says, *"if you try to hurt her, I will report you to the police."* Maxwell says, *"this isn't over Destiny!".* Destiny sighs as the guy asks, *"are you ok Destiny?".* She nods as she cries and he hands a handkerchief and says, *"I have to go but call me if you need anything".* Destiny sees the initials on the handkerchief 'KT' as she thinks, *'he seems so familiar'.*

Chapter 2

Destiny headed home thinking about the mystery man who helped her as she held the handkerchief in her hands. She was still trying to figure out who was the guy as Destiny read the two letters, *'KT'*. Destiny's mind wonders as she wanted to know who he was. she soon changed and saw Jen's laptop as there was a sticky note on it *'Use me'*. Destiny called Jen as Jen says, *"hey Destiny you ok sweetie?"*. Destiny asks, *"what's the note on your laptop?"* Jen replies, *"it will help you to find a job. I have to go speak soon."* Destiny opens and finds it is already logged in as Destiny sees a CV made for her as she begins to apply for jobs.

Destiny soon found a job advert for a company called *'KT Enterprise'*. She applied for the job and later that night after dinner got a phone call from a private number. As Destiny answered the person says, *"I am calling from KT Enterprise am I speaking with Destiny?"*. Destiny says *"speaking."* Kaiden asks, *"can you come in for an interview tomorrow at 10am?"*. Destiny replies, *"of course, thank you."* The next morning after dropping Molly off to school Destiny hurried to get home and ready for the interview. She made it with five minutes to spare. Destiny comes over to the reception desk as she says, *"hi I'm here for an interview"*. The receptionist checks on the list and replies, *"go to the top floor the CEO is waiting for you."* Destiny thanks the receptionist as she took the elevator to the top floor.

As she stood outside, she took a deep breath and knocked on Kaiden's door. *"come in"* said Kaiden. As Destiny opened the door and walked in, she saw Kaiden sitting at his desk. *"Ah Mrs. Miller, I presume."* Kaiden said. Destiny looks at Kaiden and thinks, *'I have seen him before.* Destiny sits as, corrects Kaiden and says, *"It's Miss Miller."* Kaiden conducts the interview as it finishes, and Destiny gets up to shake his hand when she remembered he saved her from Maxwell. As she is about to leave, Kaiden stops her as she turns around asking, *" is everything ok sir?."*. Kaiden replies, *"you're hired your shift starts tomorrow at 9am".* Destiny was surprised as she replied excitedly, *"thank you Mr. Turner".*

As Destiny leaves the building, she calls Jennifer at work. She says, *"guess what I got the job".* Destiny was still excited as Jennifer says, *"that's great!".* She disconnects as Destiny understands she is very busy. Later that evening Jennifer and Destiny celebrate by having pizza and non-alcoholic drinks. Destiny comes into the kitchen as she opens a drawer and sees *'KT'* handkerchief and thinks *'tomorrow I will go and return it.'* The next morning Jennifer takes Molly to school as Destiny gets ready for her first day of work. She is excited by a little nervous before leaving she takes the handkerchief. She travels on the train and comes to the building; she takes a deep breath and enters as someone says *"Miss Miller".*

Destiny is surprised to see Kaiden who says, *"you are here early."* Destiny is nervous as Kaiden says, *"it's all right it shows a very good impression".* Destiny smiles at Kaiden as Kaiden says, *"I will show you around".* Destiny says, *"sir, this belongs to you".* Kaiden laughs and says, *"you didn't have to return it, I have thousands of these handkerchiefs.."* Destiny feels sad as Kaiden says, *"it is still a lovely gesture Miss Miller, thank you".* Destiny says, *"please call me Destiny sir".*

Chapter 3

A s Kaiden apologizes to Destiny, Kaiden says, *"let me show you around the office, Destiny."* As they head up the office floor; it is quiet however people soon start coming in. Destiny asks, *"sir where is my office?".* Kaiden shows her a small cabin next to his room and says, *"your role will be my PA so you will be arranging meetings, office meetings, filing and other duties."* Destiny says, *"thank you sir".* Kaiden shows her around the staff room and also introduces her to the other members of staff.

Destiny feels happy and excited to start her new role. As she comes to her cabin, Kaiden comes and helps her set-up the computer. Destiny asks, *"sir don't you have your work to do?, I mean I don't want to take up your time."* Kaiden says, *"don't worry Destiny I am here to help you".* Destiny says, *"ok sir."* Kaiden says, *"you hate when I call you Miss Miller and I also hate the title sir, It makes me feel old."* Destiny asks, *"what would you like me to call you?".* Kaiden looks at her intensely and says, *"Kaiden or Kai".* Destiny feels a little shy, but she says, *"Kaiden sir".* Kaiden says, *"I hope one day you will be able to say my name without sir."* As Kaiden is called away; Destiny logs in and finds her email set-up as she checks the calendar.

Throughout her first day in the office Destiny is given the company policies and procedures to read and understand but also is taught about the IT filing systems. Soon the day comes to an end as all the staff head home. Destiny tells Kaiden she is leaving as Kaiden says, *"ok see you tomorrow, Destiny."* As Destiny leaves Kaiden opens his drawer as he looks at a frame photo and smiles before closing it. As Destiny comes home Molly says, *"hi mummy"*. Destiny hugs Molly and kisses her cheek as Jennifer says, *"hey Destiny"*.

Jennifer has finished cooking some shepherd pie with salad as Molly says, *"Auntie Jen is the best"*. Jennifer says, *"Molly go tidy your toys"*. Soon they all tuck in for dinner; Molly finishes as Destiny puts her on the sofa and puts the TV-show, *'Little Einsteins'*. As she heads back for dessert; Jennifer asks, *"how was your first day at work?"*. Destiny replies, *"busy but Kaiden is so sweet"*. Jennifer says, *"you mean your boss?"*. Destiny nods as she asks, *"so I wanted to ask about the divorce proceeding"*. Jennifer says, *"put Molly to sleep then we can talk more privately."*

Chapter 4

The next morning, Destiny starts filling out the divorce paper as Jennifer walks in. *"Destiny what are you doing?"* Jennifer asks. Destiny look up to see Jennifer standing there as she replies, *"filling out the forms for the divorce application".* Jennifer sat with Destiny and told her *"you will be late for work, let me manage it".* Destiny left Jennifer with the documents; at work she knew that with Maxwell gone she wanted to focus on herself. Destiny thought about Kaiden and was surprised to be thinking of him. Her memory takes her back to when they were in high-school and both Kaiden and Destiny never talked. The weekend arrived as Jennifer, Destiny and Molly had a girl's day out. After a nice weekend, another week came as Monday morning Destiny went to work; she saw Kaiden talking with a fellow employee. Destiny thought, *'are they a thing? why does it matter to me?'.* Destiny decided to focus on her work and finishes early.

She knocks on Kaiden's door as he says, *"come in".* Destiny walks in and hands Kaiden the projects and her completed work. He has a check through it and says, *"thank you Destiny, you may go home early".* Destiny walked out of his office grabbing her stuff and feeling happy on what she had achieved. Later that evening Jennifer made Mac and cheese for dinner. Jennifer says,*" I sent in your divorce papers today."* Destiny was so happy to finally get Maxwell out of her life. Destiny knew that it would take time, but she had the support of her best friend.

A few days later, Destiny got a call from the court about her divorce hearing taking place next Friday. Destiny thanks the woman as she heads to work.

She comes to Kaiden's office. Kaiden says, *"come in"*. As she sits in the chair; Kaiden asks, *"why did you come here so early?"*. Destiny takes a deep breath replying, *"Kaiden sir I need to take next Friday off."* Kaiden was surprised and asks, *"why?"*. Destiny sighs and says, *"it's the date of my divorce hearing"*. Kaiden nodded then and Destiny got up to leave; however, Kaiden says, *"Destiny hold on."* he comes around and embraces her. Destiny is surprised and stunned. Kaiden says, *"If you ever need to talk, I am here."* The next day Destiny couldn't stop thinking about the hug, Maxwell never hugged her. That day she finished her work in time before she was off; she gives the file to Kaiden who says, *"Destiny wait a second."* Destiny rushes out before dropping her keychain.

Chapter 5

K aiden looked at the keychain as Destiny had already left. Destiny comes to the school as she runs in before reaching the hall. The crowd applauds the performance as Destiny says, *"oh no!"*. As they enjoy the spread Molly sees Destiny as she looks upset. Jennifer sees Destiny as Jennifer says, *"Destiny, Molly was amazing"*. Destiny says, *"I tried to get here as soon I can."* Destiny looks at Molly who doesn't look happy. As they come home Molly heads upstairs as Destiny tries to talk to her. Jennifer says, *"you need to make it up to her"*. Destiny empties her bag as she tries to find the keychain and wonders what has happened to it.

Kaiden is at home with the keychain as someone comes in and says, *"Kai-kai"*. Kaiden turns to see a woman dressed hot in lingerie. Kaiden says, *"I am tired babes."* Meanwhile, at home Destiny wondered how she could make it up to Molly. A few days later, Destiny has promised a special day with Molly. At work Destiny works hard to complete all the tasks as she finishes; Kaiden calls out, *" Destiny."* Destiny says, *"sorry Kaiden sir"*. Kaiden says, *"a few days ago you disappeared quickly. Is everything ok?"* Destiny replies, *"I have to go for an appointment"*. Kaiden says, *"ok"*. Destiny comes down quickly, she trips. The security guard calls Kaiden. Kaiden rushes down as Destiny says painfully, *"my ankle"*. Kaiden lifts her and brings her to the nurse's room. Destiny says, *"Kaiden I need to go"*.

Kaiden smiled hearing Destiny say his name without sir. The nurse checks her ankle and says, *"it's a small sprain."* The nurse wraps the injury. Destiny says, *"I won't be able to drive."* Kaiden says, *"I will drive you."* Destiny says, *"I don't want to bother you."* Kaiden says, *"it's fine."*

Kaiden drives Destiny to the school. Molly sees her and comes; Destiny says, *"come on Molly."* Molly sees Kaiden as she asks, *"who are you?"*. Kaiden replies, *"call me Kay".* Molly laughs and says, *"okay."* Destiny says, *"guess what we are going to the zoo?"*. Molly cheers and is so happy and excited. At the Zoo, Molly is excited seeing all the animals. Molly says, *"Mommy lift me I want to see the giraffe".* Destiny tries to hold Molly but is unable to; Kaiden lifts her and puts her on his shoulder.

She laughs and smiles. Destiny says, *"thanks".* Kaiden treats Destiny in the café with some delicious food as Molly enjoys the trip. As they go into the gift shop Molly sees a beautiful teddy giraffe. Destiny says, *"Molly you can choose something else."* Kaiden says, *"Molly take it."* Kaiden paid for it as Destiny thanked him. Kaiden says, *"you consider me your friend, right?"*. Destiny says, *"you are my boss Kaiden."* Kaiden smiles as Destiny says, *"you have been smiling a lot today."* Kaiden say, *"you said my name without sir."* Destiny was shy as Kaiden says, *"it's nice."* Destiny blushes as Molly soon feels tired and Kaiden says, *"I will drop you both home."*

Chapter 6

Kaiden drives Destiny and Molly home. Molly run inside leaving Destiny with Kaiden alone; Destiny smiles whilst Kaiden is unsure and a little nervous of what to say. Kaiden look at ground and then back at her asking, *"do you even remember me?"* Destiny looks surprised by his question replying, *"what do you mean Kaiden?."* She entered the house before thanking Kaiden and closing the door; Kaiden came back to his car and was in deep thoughts and drove off. Inside Molly had finished seeing Kaiden and Destiny outside. *"mommy, are you cheating on daddy?"* asked Molly. Destiny was shocked by Molly's word and replies, *"no honey I'm not, come on its late time for bed,"* said Destiny. After a long day Molly and Destiny soon fell asleep.

The next morning, Destiny sat Molly down and says, *"your dad will not be around anymore."* Molly looked at Destiny confused asking, *"what do you mean mommy?."* Destiny says with tears in her eyes, *"we are getting divorce tomorrow."* Molly starts to cry and says, *"daddy was always bad to us it's for the best, right mommy?."* Destiny looks at Molly hugging her daughter and thought, *'I am so happy my daughter is so understanding.'*

The day went quickly as soon it was the divorce hearing. Destiny was getting ready to finally get rid of Maxwell forever; Jennifer helps Destiny with the final preparations. Molly was at school not knowing what was happening. Outside the courtroom, Destiny waited and soon saw Kaiden as she was surprised asking, *"what are you doing here, boss?."* Kaiden smiled and replied, *"I am here to support you".* They saw the judge entering, Maxwell came and glared angrily at Destiny as he entered the courtroom. Destiny took a deep breath as Kaiden says, *"you've got this"*. Destiny nodded and entered the court.

Chapter 7

The judge sits as Maxwell shoots a glare at Destiny. The judge says, *"please begin with divorce case".* Jennifer who is representing Destiny says, *"your honour my client Destiny has been subjected to years of neglect and abuse not just on the relationship of their marriage but also their daughter".* Maxwell says, *"that's a lie!".* The judge bangs its gravel and says, *"order please!".* The defendant says, *"Maxwell is an upstanding citizen and individual".* Jennifer says, *"your honour I would like to call Destiny to the stand".* Destiny stands and goes to the box; Maxwell is called to the other box; they are face to face but opposite side.

Destiny says, *"your honour my daughter Molly has been left in his care a few times and he left her to starve and neglected her".* Maxwell says, *"the brat was constantly whining, I never wanted kids.".* Everyone was shocked by Maxwell's talk continuing to insult both Molly and Destiny; Kaiden was angry and thought, *'How could he say such things about his daughter?'.* Destiny says, *"your true color has been revealed Maxwell, marrying you was the biggest mistake of my life; honestly Molly deserves better."* The judge says, *"we will adjourn this case for a small recess".* Outside Kaiden brings Destiny a coffee as Maxwell sees them and says, *"look who it is, my cheating wife with the scum!"* Kaiden felt angry and wanted to punch Maxwell however Destiny held him back. Destiny says, *"you're a spiteful and lowlife Max!".* Maxwell was about to hit her when Kaiden punched him saying, *"YOU BASTARD! How dare you try to raise your hand on her!".* The court case resumes as Destiny comes back inside with Kaiden as Maxwell has a bruised eye as the judge asks, *"what happened?"*. Destiny replies, *"he tried to hit me your honour but in self-defence Kaiden protected me"*.

Jennifer and the defendant continue to bring more evidence and documentation regarding the case as the judge says, *"I have seen and heard enough to say that in this case the favour of Destiny; your divorce application is accepted and also the custody of your daughter Molly will be solely yours Destiny"*. Destiny was happy whilst Maxwell left fuming. Destiny came out as Jennifer hugged her and congratulated her on the divorce. Destiny smiled as Kaiden says, *"you did it!"*. Destiny happily hugs Kaiden and thanks him for his support. Kaiden smiles thinking, 'I *will always be here for you Destiny'.* Jennifer says, *"we need to celebrate this."* Destiny asks, *"Kaiden will you join us?"*. Kaiden replies, *"only if you want me to."* Destiny smiled as Kaiden looks at her smiling back.

Chapter 8

They drove to a restaurant to celebrate; Destiny and Kaiden are laughing, and they had amazing time. Destiny give a speech about being free from Maxwell as Jennifer says, *"I am so happy to have my bestie back."*. Jennifer says, *"a toast to Destiny!"*, they all raise their glasses and lightly clink it. Kaiden's phone soon rings as he says, *"excuse me ladies"*. He gets up and heads outside answering the call. As Kaiden says, *"hey Amelia"*. Amelia asks, *"babes where are you?"*. Kaiden replies, *"just finishing work stuff I will be home soon."*. Kaiden ends the call and comes back in.

Destiny asks, *"is everything okay Kaiden?"*. Kaiden replies, *"yes I have to get home."* Jennifer says, *"thanks for being there for Destiny today."* Kaiden says to Destiny, *"sure see you tomorrow at work."* Destiny smiled as Kaiden left as Jennifer noticed and says, *"don't tell me you have the hots for your boss!"*. Destiny embarrassed says, *"Jen"*. As Kaiden opened the door he put the light on and saw rose petals on the floor. He went into the living room and saw candles with two delicious foods as Amelia was wearing a red lingerie. Amelia says, *"I made your favourite food babes!"*

Kaiden says, *"I am not hungry; I am going to work in the study"*. Amelia was confused and felt annoyed that all her preparations went to waste. Kaiden came to his study closing the door as he put the light on and opened his drawer to a photo-album he knew that he would have to tell Destiny the truth soon and who he was. As he opened the photo album, he stroked the girl's photo and smiled. It was Destiny and

Kaiden when they were younger. Kaiden had an idea and takes one of the photos and adds it to a frame wrapped up to give to Destiny.

The next day at work Kaiden waited in the office as Destiny rushed in early. Kaiden says, *"Destiny what a pleasant surprise!"*. Destiny says, *"I am sorry I...."* Kaiden says, *"I hope you are ready."* Destiny looked a little confused as Kaiden handed her a file for their overnight conference. Destiny then got a call from Jennifer that Maxwell had got arrested for DUI. Destiny says, *"he's not my problem anymore."* Destiny told Kaiden about Maxwell as he laughed. Kaiden says, *"let's go!"*. Destiny says, *"wait I didn't bring any clothes."* As they come down to the car; Destiny sees two packed suitcases. Kaiden says, *"I don't normally do ladies shopping."* Destiny thanks Kaiden as he smiles.

Meanwhile Amelia was busy with arranging the engagement party invitations. Kaiden and Destiny headed on the trip as Destiny stopped the car as Kaiden asked, *"what happened Destiny?"*. Destiny opens the door as she steps out. Kaiden comes out as the driver opens an umbrella. Destiny comes near a hill as the rain pours down. She smiles as she spins and dances happily. Kaiden watches her as Destiny pulls Kaiden's hand and holds him as she dances. They share an eye lock as the thunder booms. Destiny is about to slip when Kaiden holds her. Destiny says, *"I wanted to feel the rain forever."* Kaiden thinks, *'I wish I could hold you forever.'*

Chapter 9

They get back in the car as they drive off to the conference. At the conference after a long meeting Kaiden and Destiny are both in their room. As they are both unable to sleep Kaiden comes and knocks on Destiny's door. Destiny opens to see Kaiden asking, *"is everything ok Kaiden I mean sir?"*. Kaiden nods and says, *"actually I couldn't sleep so I was wondering if you wanted to order room service and watch a movie."* Destiny says, *"sure"*. She comes over to his room and it is a big suite as she sits on the bed and Kaiden orders the food as Destiny asks, *"how do you know what I will like?"*. Kaiden smiles and says, *"I don't know what you will like I am ordering my favourite foods."* Destiny laughs and then hits Kaiden with a pillow. Kaiden sees the DVD he has and says, *"we have Harry potter and the chamber of secrets or the notebook."* Destiny says, *"two great choices."* Destiny says, *"I love Harry potter let's watch that."* As Kaiden puts it on; he says, *"I was sure you would have chosen the notebook movie."* Destiny laughs and says, *"yeah but I am full of surprises"*.

The room service comes in as Kaiden tips the staff and brings it in. As Destiny who is starving sees the food. She smiles and says, *"chicken chow mein, fish ball dumplings, stir fry rice"*. Kaiden says, *"I am a huge fan of Chinese food. It's my favourite."* Destiny says, *"I love Chinese food too."* Kaiden serves Destiny as they both sit on the bed eating the food and watching Harry potter and the Chamber of secrets. As they eat Kaiden spills some food around his mouth as Destiny laughs and tries to help him as she uses a cloth to clean it. Kaiden feels her warmth as she says, *"you're a messy eater."* Destiny sees red wine and two glasses as she feels a little hesitant to drink as Kaiden says, *"don't worry I won't force you to drink or anything."* Kaiden pours himself a glass and drinks; a scary scene comes in the Harry Potter movie as Destiny grabs the wine and drinks it. As the movie finishes, she gets up and starts dancing as Kaiden finds it funny; Destiny is about to fall as Kaiden holds her, and they share an eyelock. Destiny closes her eyes as she passes out due to the drink. Kaiden places her on the bed and covers her with the blanket.

The next morning Destiny awakes and sees breakfast as Kaiden is dressed and says, *"we are going to explore the town."* Kaiden and Destiny explored the town as Kaiden takes pictures of Destiny as he smiles at her. Destiny spots a tattoo artist who mistakes them as a couple as Destiny says, *"I always wished to do something exciting".* Kaiden is nervous about doing it as Destiny asks, *"if I get a tattoo would you get one done Kaiden sir?".* Destiny says, *"I wanted to get an initial".* As the tattoo artist takes Destiny's hand, she gets a *'K'* initial onto her finger. Kaiden's hand is also pulled as he gets a *'D'* on his finger too. They both look at each other. As they soon head back Kaiden tries to wash it off as Destiny feels a little embarrassed by it. Destiny apologises for the tattoo as Kaiden says, *"it's ok don't worry."* Meanwhile Jennifer is with Molly at a café as Maxwell approaches them. Molly calls out *'Daddy';* Maxwell tries to make a scene as Jennifer takes Molly away. Later that evening as Kaiden and Destiny are on their way home they are both lost in thoughts of each other.

Chapter 10

Destiny and Kaiden come back into town as both are in deep thoughts; Destiny walks on her way home and thinks, *'why can't I stop thinking about him?'*. Kaiden walked in the opposite direction he also was in thought over Destiny, *'why can't I stop thinking about her?'*. Kaiden soon reached home, saw Amelia waiting for him and they shared a hug. Kaiden had a cup of tea as Amelia says, *"babes let's go to bed"*. Kaiden says, *"I am not feeling that tired, you go and sleep."* Destiny reached home as she saw Molly and Jennifer asleep on the couch and spotted a cake on the table *'Welcome home Mommy!'*. Destiny had a shower and went to sleep. The next morning early at the office Kaiden placed the envelope on each person's desk. As everyone came in and saw the envelope and were talking about it. The engagement was only two days away. The next day Destiny walked to Kaiden's office as she knocks with Kaiden saying, *"come in"*. Destiny comes in and says, *"sir why is everyone acting crazy today sir?"*. Kaiden was cold to her replying, *"I've got work to do Destiny"*. Destiny feels a little sad because of Kaiden's response towards her and leaves the room.

Two days came quickly as the engagement party was above the office on the balcony that evening which had been decorated. As everyone is gathered at the party; Kaiden is wearing a black tux as Amelia is wearing a red and gold dress. Amelia remembers something and asks Kaiden; *"babes, I think you left something at your office"*. Destiny was on her way to the office as Kaiden calls her and says, *"before you come up can you grab something I left in my office."* Destiny nods and says, *"of course sir"*. Destiny comes to building and reaches the office where she comes into Kaiden's room as she starts to look around, she soon notices a wrapped present on top of the shelf as it was addressed to her. Destiny brings it upstairs as she comes to the top floor, she sees the party in full swing. Destiny gives Kaiden the document as she goes to the corner holding the present addressed to her. Kaiden sees her and wonders, *'how did Destiny find the wrapped photo?'*. Kaiden rushes off to stop her however Destiny opens it and sees a framed photo of a young boy and girl together. Destiny looked at the picture and recognizes the girl as she thinks, *'this is me when I was young but who is this boy?'*.

Destiny looked at Kaiden as she asked showing the framed photo, *"who is this boy in the photo beside me?"*. Kaiden took a deep breath and replied, *"it's me we used to be childhood friends."* Destiny was shocked as Amelia came over to Kaiden holding her arm and says, *"babes we need to go exchange rings now"*. Kaiden left with Amelia who looked around at the press and everyone, she was excited however as she was about to make Kaiden wear the ring he saw the *'D'* tattoo on his finger. Amelia dropped the ring as she asked Kaiden, *"whose name is D and why is it tattooed on your finger? are you cheating on me?"*. Kaiden looked at Amelia and didn't know how to respond. Amelia was hurt and angry as she slapped Kaiden and left as the weather in the sky changed; Kaiden and Destiny looked at each other.

Chapter 11

K aiden and Destiny looked at each as the weather begins to get thundery above them. The guests began to leave as Kaiden said, *"Destiny there's no one to stop us from being together."* Destiny felt anger as she replies, *"How could you say that? You broke Amelia's heart. I can't be the second woman in your life."* Kaiden says, *"fate would have broken me and Amelia apart. I thought I had loved her, but I didn't."* Destiny looks sadly at Kaiden and says, *"do you know what it feels like to be with someone stuck in a relationship with no love? Me and Maxwell relationship was fake but Molly she is real."* Kaiden says, *"Destiny I love you and I accept you and Molly."* Kaiden came closer to Destiny who had tears in her eyes however before Kaiden could wipe her tears a person grabbed Kaiden from behind. Destiny was shocked and stunned to see it was Amelia. The weather became stormy as Amelia angrily yells; *"YOU CHEATED AND LIED TO ME. OUR WHOLE RELATIONSHIP WAS FAKE. HOW COULD YOU DO THIS TO ME?"* Amelia slapped Kaiden as he says, *"I deserve this. I can't control my heart and I have loved Destiny forever; I'm sorry."*

Amelia's brother Lee grabbed Kaiden's collar and said, *"YOU BROKE MY SISTER'S HEART."* He began to beat Kaiden badly as Destiny was about to go over when Amelia pulled her wrist turning her to face her. Amelia says, *"Look at you. you think you are some mystical angel that can attract any man. YOU ARE NOTHING MORE THAN A BITCH!"* Amelia slapped Destiny as Maxwell came there. Destiny saw him drunk as Destiny asks, *"Maxwell what are you doing here?".* Maxwell grabbed Destiny's arm as he says, *"you're coming with me";*

Kaiden saw what was happening and punched Lee off. Maxwell tried to drag Destiny as Kaiden came between them. Destiny cries, *"Kaiden."* Kaiden pulls Destiny away as he says, *"MAXWELL YOU SCUM HOW DARE YOU GO NEAR HER?".* Maxwell says, *"You are the cause of all the problems! I WILL KILL YOU."* Maxwell and Kaiden fight as Maxwell hits a glass bottle over Kaiden's head. Destiny screams, *"KAIDEN."* The storm begins to get worse as a small flood of water begins to soak the rooftop.

Amelia and Lee leave as Maxwell sees Destiny run towards Kaiden who is unconscious. Destiny places Kaiden's head near her heart as she cries and says, *"Kaiden please be ok."* Maxwell grabs Destiny telling her to come with him as Kaiden's body falls to the floor. Destiny pushes Maxwell as she shouts, *"ENOUGH! I AND YOU ARE OVER! I WISH I NEVER MET YOU. I WISH I HAD A SECOND CHANCE TO START THINGS AGAIN! YOU ARE MY LIFE'S WORST MISTAKE."* The storm heavies rain above as the flood becomes deeper as Destiny calls Kaiden's name. As she is turned, she is unaware Maxwell has stabbed her back with a broken glass bottle as he says, *"YOU DESERVE THIS BITCH!".* Destiny drops to the floor as she closes her eyes in pain as her mouth bleeds blood. she steps backward over the rail she is about to fall when someone grabs her hand. She opens her eyes and sees it is Kaiden. Kaiden says, *"Destiny you will be ok; I am going to pull you up."* Destiny remembers her moments with Kaiden as he tries to assure her she will be ok. Destiny blocks out all thoughts as she closes her eyes and thinks ' *if only had a second chance to rewrite my destiny. It's said that the rain holds the power to wishes but will this happen?'.* Destiny says, *"I love you Kaiden."* She lets go and falls back with Kaiden watching her and screaming her name in pain.

Destiny closes her eyes and soon sees she has stopped falling. She opens her eyes and sees it is a space-like cloud surrounding her. Destiny sees herself in white clothes with no injury she wonders, *'am I dead?'.* A woman comes to Destiny with wings holding a book. The angel says, *"I am your guardian angel Richelle. I know you have had a hard life Destiny and you made a wish before you died."* Destiny asks, *"what will happen to me? will I become an angel?".* Richelle smiles and answers, *"no you will have a second chance to live, to find your true love however if you are unable to change your life before the end of six months you will die."* Destiny notices the *'K'* tattoo on her finger is gone as Richelle says, *"you will not have any memory of your present life."* Destiny had many questions however Richelle opened her book chanting a spell; *'send her back, erase all past, give a second chance to undo all. Rewrite her fate and new life.'* Richelle blew a small white ball towards Destiny as everything soon went white.

Early the next morning a voice calls out *'Destiny... Destiny'.* The young woman awakes in her PJs as her golden hair is still perfect and comes to the bathroom. As she looks at herself, she smiles as she showers and changes wearing a blue striped top and black skinny jeans. As she comes down, she says, *"hi mom something smells delicious."* Isabelle says, *"you are up early for a change."* Jennifer says, *"finally Destiny you are here. I am so looking for our first day of college."* Destiny smiled as she grabbed a toast and ate it.

Chapter 12

After breakfast, Destiny and Jennifer walk to school. Jen asks, *"Are you excited for the first day of college?"*. Destiny nods, *"of course, I have a feeling this year will be a year to remember"*. They soon reach Fairwood College entrance a voice calls out *'Destiny'*. Destiny turns as she sees a guy with brown slicked back hairstyle wearing a black leather jacket with green eyes as Destiny says, *"Maxwell."* Jennifer rolls her eyes as she walks in as Destiny walks down the steps and shares a hug with Maxwell. Maxwell says, *"I missed you over the holiday babes."* Just as they are about to catch up the bell rings as Destiny says, *"I don't want to be late for class especially on the first day of college."* Maxwell kisses Destiny as he says, *"I'll see you at lunch babes."* Destiny heads to the classroom as Jennifer moves her bag as Destiny says, *"thanks Jen".* A young man in a suit enters the classroom as he says, *"good morning students and I hope you are all excited for a new term. I will be your tutor Mr. Asterwell."* Jennifer says, *"it's going to be a long morning."* Destiny smiles as the morning classes finish quicker than expected.

In the canteen Maxwell is with his friends at the table laughing as Destiny comes in. Maxwell sees Destiny and says, *"babes come over".* Destiny comes over to the table as Maxwell introduces her as his girlfriend. Maxwell says, *"I'll see you guys later."* Maxwell and Destiny sneak out the back of the college as Destiny says, *"Maxwell I have classes in the afternoon."* Maxwell brings her to a restaurant nearby as Destiny looks around and thinks, *'I am too underdressed for this restaurant.'* Maxwell and Destiny sit at a table as Maxwell asks for the menu. Destiny looks around as Maxwell asks, *"babes have you chosen what you want to eat?".* Destiny looks at the menu and chooses the burger and chips. Maxwell laughs and says, *"babes I brought you to a fancy restaurant not for burger and chips."* Maxwell tells the waiter to bring two steaks as Destiny says, *"really Maxwell? I am not that hungry".* Maxwell holds her hand as he says, *"I only want to give you the best babes."* After finishing their meals Destiny is about to leave checking the time on her watch as Maxwell holds her hand and gives her a small, wrapped box with a golden bow. Destiny takes it as she asks, *"what is this, Maxwell?".* Maxwell smiles as he says, *"open it".* Destiny opens it, she sees a silver locket as she opens to find hers and Maxwell's photo. Maxwell says, *"happy anniversary babes."* Maxwell says, *"I will make you wear it."* As she stands up, he ties it on her neck. Just as they are about to kiss Destiny's phone rings.

Destiny sees Jen's incoming call as she says, *"Maxwell I have to head back to class."* Destiny thanks Maxwell for the gift and kisses him on the cheek before leaving. As Destiny comes back to the college Jennifer asks, *"where were you?".* Destiny says, *"let's just have a girl's day out after college".* Jennifer nodded as the class began. Soon time flew quickly as after school Maxwell was waiting for Destiny as Jennifer rolled her eyes and thought, *'I knew it Destiny is going to blow me off'.* Destiny comes over to Maxwell as he has his bike ready. Destiny says, *"babes I'm going to spend the rest of the day with Jen".* Maxwell noticed Jen as he hugged Destiny who says, *"I'll see you tomorrow."* Maxwell gave Jen a cold stare as Jen rolled her eyes. Maxwell drove off as Destiny came to Jen and asked, *"are you ready for our girl's day out?".* They caught the bus and went into town. Jen and Destiny spent hours in the mall shopping for new outfits and getting some beauty therapy. They soon sat down in a posh café Jen asks, *"so you never told me where you were at lunch?".* Destiny replies, *"oh yeah. Maxwell took me to a fancy restaurant, and he also got me a gift."* As they both enjoyed their afternoon teas; evening soon came, and Destiny walked Jen home. Jen says, *"I'll see you tomorrow."* Destiny nodded and left as she came home, she put her shopping bags in the corner and jumped into the shower before falling asleep.

Chapter 13

The next day Destiny awoke, got changed and saw Jen waiting for her downstairs. As they walked to school Jen was talking about the extracurricular activities as Destiny was in deep thoughts. Jen clicked finger and said, *"earth to Destiny?"*. Destiny came out of her thoughts and replied *"huh."* Jen says, *"where were you? you looked like you were in your own word."* Destiny says, *"don't worry."* Destiny thinks, *'it's better if I don't tell Jen. She might think I am being crazy or acting like a weirdo.'* As they come to college Jen and Destiny enter, Maxwell was by Destiny's locker. Jen says, *"I'll see you in class."* Destiny came over to the locker as Maxwell stood against it and says, *"hey Babes I missed you."* Destiny kissed Maxwell as the bell rang again as Maxwell says, *"this bell always ruins our romance."* Maxwell says, *"I'll see you at practice later."* Destiny nods. At lunchtime Jen and Destiny go to the try-outs for the cheerleading team. Jen says, *"it will feel just like in school."* Destiny smiles excitedly. Soon they stand with the group of girls waiting for the try-outs to begin. Destiny feels nervous as she thinks, *'why do I feel so nervous? I've got this.'* Just then a girl with red hair wearing a cheerleading squad outfit came with two other girls beside her. Jen whispered to Destiny, *'those two must be her minions.'* As the red hair girl said, *"welcome to try-outs, this year is an important year at Fairwood, and I want the team to be the best. In case you all must be wondering I'm Naomi and these two girls beside me are Michelle and Kitty."* Jen and Destiny began to warm up with the other girls as Destiny still was feeling a little absent-minded.

After practicing and warmups, Naomi said, *"so first we will have solo cheerleading dance and finally a choregraph one."* As the girls one by one did a solo Naomi, Michelle and Kitty had to make a lot of cuts before a small group was selected. Just then onto the field the football team came on the pitch as Naomi turned to see the girls spotting Maxwell. Maxwell noticed Destiny and waved at her as Naomi waved to him. Kitty says, *"Maxwell is so hot."* Michelle says, *"yeah but he's off limit."* Naomi said, *"girls stop gossiping".* As they turned back to the girls Naomi demonstrated the choregraphed dance for the finale as Destiny was the lightest of the girls as Naomi pointed at Destiny said, *"You will be the top of the pyramid".* Jen says, *"she has a name. you know not just 'you'".* The girls laughed as Naomi came over to Jen and said, *"names are irrelevant unless you make the squad."* Jen wanted to argue back but Destiny said, *"leave it out Jen."* Michelle put the music on the girls dance before doing the finale of pyramid with Destiny on top. As Destiny was on top, she sees a small white figure; Destiny didn't know why but she felt something but confused too as she couldn't hold her balance and fell with the other girls. Naomi came over and said, *"you girl what's your name?".* Destiny replied, *"I'm Destiny."* Naomi rolled her eyes and said to her and Jen, *"unfortunately you two don't meet the criteria of what I am looking for."*

Jen was not happy as she helped Destiny up. Destiny looked around to see if the figure was there however it was not as she thought, *'is my mind playing tricks on me?'.* Jen brought Destiny to the nurse's room. Destiny felt a small pain in her ankle as the nurse advised her to rest for a few days. Jen says, *"I can't believe Naomi had the nerve to cut us both. We were two of the best at try-outs."* The nurse who was a kind woman asked, *"you two were trying out for the team?".* Destiny nodded and said, *"me and Jen were co-captain at our school."* The nurse says, *"that's great actually my husband Rick is the coach of the sports department."* She told them more as Jen had a plan. Soon, Destiny came out with her ankle bandaged, she saw Maxwell. Maxwell asks, *"Destiny are you ok?"*. Destiny nodded as Maxwell lifted her as Destiny felt a little embarrassed. He carried her to class as Naomi and her friends watched her. Naomi said, *"Maxwell why are you lifting her? she only fell in try-outs."* Maxwell says, *"she's my girlfriend and I need to make sure she's ok."* Naomi felt anger as she thought, *'I will make you mine Maxwell.'* Throughout the rest of the day Maxwell stayed beside Destiny's side like a hawk helping her. Destiny did come out on the pitch to see if she could find the mystery figure she saw. She wondered about it and then a thought came to her mind, *'I need to go the place'.*

Chapter 14

After school that evening Destiny came to the place, she had been thinking about. As she held a candle in her hand, walked down the church and looked around at the color glass of God. She lighted the candle as she bent down on her knees holding her hand in a prayer as she thought, *so many strange things have been happening lately; I don't know what to do. why do I have a feeling of doubt about Maxwell? you know we have been together for many years. Show me a sign and guide me. Amen!*. Destiny got up, she noticed a white figure that was watching her as Destiny rubbed her eyes as she said, *"you can't be real. Just a figment of my imagination."* Richelle replied, *"honey I'm real; always with you."* Before Destiny can say anything else; someone enters the church as Richelle disappears. Soon, Destiny walked out from the church, she didn't see the mystery-guy face however she turned back looking at God and thought, *'whatever this guy wishes for. Please help him too'.*

Destiny comes out of church and sees Jen waiting for her. Jen said, *"Destiny I knew you must be here."* Destiny hugged Jen as they walked home. Destiny felt hungry and Jen said, *"I know just the place Italian Bistro."* After eating Destiny stays over at Jen's house for the night as she has a strange dream of an unknown guy. As she wakes up for a moment looking around, she thinks, *'I shouldn't worry.'* The next few days at college Destiny focused on her studies as Maxwell comes and says, *"babes are you avoiding me?"*. Destiny said, *" I've been busy with study."* Jen went to speak with the coach regarding cheerleading practice. Destiny and Maxwell had lunch in the canteen. Naomi along with her friends watched them as Naomi said, *"what's special about her? Maxwell could have me."* Destiny came to the counter to get some juice as Naomi whispered to her friend who went over and pushed Destiny. The students gathered around taking pictures and laughing; Maxwell came in, saw Destiny, and helped her up. Maxwell asked, *"who is responsible for this?"*. Destiny replies, *"forget it I'm fine."*

Destiny walked home as she noticed the house across had been sold. Destiny came in as she asked, *"mom did you know the house across us has been sold?"*. Isabelle replied, *"that's nice sweetie. how's college?"*. In the house across the street, the mystery guy was the same person from the church as he was in his room setting it up. A voice called him, *"Kaiden come and help me with this"*. Kaiden came downstairs to see his mom Marie and Daniel trying to put a frame up as Kaiden helped as Marie said, *"thanks son."* Kaiden asked, *"mom, Dad is there anything else you need?"*. Marie and Daniel both shaked their head as Kaiden headed back to his room and began sorting out the box. He then found a photo-frame as he hanged it up of a young girl and boy. Kaiden thought, *'Destiny wherever you are right now; I hope you are still amazing.'* As the Turner family settle in, Isabelle heads over one evening with a pie to welcome the new neighbours. Marie opens the door to Isabelle as Marie says *"Isa"*. Isabelle's smile grew as she said, *"Mars."* Isabelle came in, puts the pie down and hugged Marie; Marie and Isabelle catches up as Daniel enters.

Chapter 15

D aniel came in to see Marie with Isabelle. Isabelle said, *"hi Daniel."* They both shared a hug as Daniel asked, *"where's Richard? I can't believe I am seeing you after so many years."* Isabelle said, *"Richard's on a business trip as always."* Marie said, *"Isa came over to drop a pie and she lives over the road."* As the two friends catch-up, Isa looks at the time and said, *"I better get home, but we should do dinner soon."* Kaiden came in as he headed to his room. The next day Destiny came to the café as Kaiden was also there as Destiny ordered her favourite latte however Kaiden accidentally bumps into Destiny as she screams, and the latte is all over her outfit. Destiny said, *"you idiot."* Kaiden tries to help her; his phone rings as he heads out. Destiny doesn't see his face feeling annoyed and thinks, *'what a jerk'.* Destiny comes out as people laugh at her in the street when Jen comes and asks, *"woah what happened?".* Destiny replies, *"some jerk bumped into me and didn't even apologise."* Jen said, *"you can't come to college like this."* Destiny sighs as she heads home to get change.

Destiny puts her clothes in the wash and changes. Destiny sees Maxwell's incoming call. She answers as she says, *"hey Maxwell."* Maxwell asks, *"hey babes where are you?".* Destiny said, *"I am on my way, see you soon."* As Destiny heads to class, she sees Naomi sitting with Maxwell. The teacher decides to pair everyone in partners as Jen is paired with another guy as Destiny is by herself; Naomi said, *"looks like everyone has a pair except for deluded Destiny."* As her friends laughed Maxwell looked at Naomi and said, *"I won't be partnered with a bully."* The teacher said, *"unfortunately the pairs have been confirmed but*

Naomi you will receive detention for bullying your classmate." At home Kaiden was chilling as Marie came calling, *"Kaiden."* Kaiden got up asking, *"mom are you ok?".* Marie gave him a letter replying, *"you will be starting Fairwood College tomorrow."* Back in college as everyone left the class; Destiny stayed back and spoke with the teacher. However, Ms Rosewell said, *"Destiny don't worry. A new student will be starting tomorrow, and he will be your partner."* Jen waited for Destiny who said, *" this evening we have another trial."* Destiny was nervous for the cheerleading trial Jen assured her; she would be ok.

Later after college, Destiny and Jen were ready with a few girls for the cheerleading squad try out as Naomi was in detention her two friends were watching the team as the coach said, *"I would like Jen and Destiny to lead the team for this try-out."* Destiny and Jen played music as everyone formed the pyramid and everyone was on point. The coach was impressed as he said, *"I think we have our new captains for the cheerleading squad."* Destiny and Jen were happy however Naomi's friend went to go and inform her. Naomi screamed, *"WHAT????*
HOW DARE THAT WANNABE STEAL MY POSITION?". Kaiden enters Fairwood College and comes to the admission department. The coach congratulates Destiny and Jen on their new position. As Destiny said, *"I can't believe we are team captains."* Naomi planned with her two friends. As Destiny and Jen walked past the admission department; Kaiden felt a strong feeling as he turned to see the corridor was empty as he thought *'why did it feel like someone was close to me?'.*

Chapter 16

Kaiden comes home after completing his admission to the college; Marie says, *"son I made your favourite chicken pie and mash potatoes."* Kaiden eats his dinner and soon heads upstairs as he relaxes on his bed. Meanwhile, Destiny was in her room in thoughts as she looked at the stars from her window as she closed her eyes and made a wish. The next morning, Destiny was about to enter class however Naomi blocked the door and says, *"Destiny".* Destiny looked at Naomi asking, *"can I please get past Naomi?".* Naomi lets her past, however, trips Destiny who is about to fall when someone holds her. As Maxwell, Jen and the teacher come inside. Destiny sees the person who has saved her from falling. He helps her up and asks, *"are you ok?".* Destiny nods and replies, *"thanks for helping me."* The teacher said, *"ah Kaiden please come to the front."* Kaiden comes to the front; Jen comes next to Destiny as she asked, *"what happened? who's the new guy?".* Destiny said, *"I'll explain after class."* Naomi and her minions call Kaiden a geek. Kaiden replies, *"at least I am not a bully like you. pushing a girl over."* The teacher introduces Kaiden as he goes to sit at the back. Destiny turns thinking, *'why does he look so familiar?'.* After class Destiny tells Jen what Naomi did and how Kaiden had saved her.

Kaiden comes out; Destiny introduces herself, *"hi I'm Destiny and this is my best friend, Jen."* Kaiden extends his hand and Destiny shakes it as she feels a strong connection however Maxwell comes beside Destiny and holds her waist as he kisses her cheek and said, *"hey babe."* Maxwell said, *"you must be the newbie in our class. stay away from my girl."* As Maxwell takes Destiny away; Kaiden sighs as Jen says *"please excuse maxwell. He's her boyfriend. As you are new; would you like a tour of the campus?".* Kaiden nods as Jen takes him on a tour around the college. Meanwhile, Naomi was with her two friends and said, *"we need to make a plan to do three things; get back my captaincy on the cheerleading squad, humiliate destiny and steal Maxwell."* As the girls discuss in a private room. Kaiden looks around the campus as it is big and feels friendly. Kaiden passes the gym as he notices on the noticeboard of extracurricular activities. Jen says, *"there are many clubs we do like soccer, rugby, basketball, dance, and more."* Meanwhile, Maxwell brought Destiny to his private spot and began to kiss her passionately however Destiny stopped Maxwell and said, *"I am not in the mood for this."* Maxwell said, *"babes are you ok? Why do I feel like you've been avoiding me?".* Destiny sighed as she left leaving Maxwell in deep thoughts.

Destiny comes to look for Jen who is with Kaiden. Destiny sees Kaiden she apologizes for Maxwell; Kaiden says, *"it's ok."* The bell rings for the next class as the teacher starts the lesson and comes to Destiny saying, *"you will be partnered with Kaiden for the team project."* Naomi was with Maxwell studying as Kaiden sat next to Destiny and began to work on the project. Destiny thought, *'he seems like such a cool guy.'* The morning classes were quick as Kaiden came to the canteen for each lunch with Destiny coming in with Jen. Destiny noticed the back of Kaiden's head. Destiny said, *"where have I seen him before?".* Jen said, *"Destiny, he's a new student."* Destiny thought for a moment and soon said, *"he's the guy who spilled coffee on me a few days ago."* Jen asked, *"are you sure Destiny?".* As Maxwell overheard the conversation, he went up to Kaiden and threw his coke over Kaiden; Destiny and Jen were shocked by this.

Chapter 17

K aiden's glasses fell, and he dropped his tray as he wiped his face; Maxwell said, *"that's for spilling coffee over my girl."* Destiny and Jen come over as Jen help Kaiden as Destiny asks, *"Kaiden are you ok?".* Kaiden gets up he grabs his bag and runs out of the canteen. Destiny said, *"what the hell Maxwell? How could you do that to Kaiden?".* Maxwell said, *"he deserved it. he spilled coffee on you."* Destiny then went to someone and said, *"wipe your hamburger on my face."* The guy is reluctant to do it; Destiny does it herself as Maxwell's anger boils. Before he can do anything; Destiny holds his hand and says, *"enough maxwell! It was an accident, and I would have sorted it myself. not only have you humiliated Kaiden; you have also hurt me."* Destiny grabs a tissue, sees Kaiden's glasses on the floor grabbing them and runs out of the canteen. Maxwell is in thoughts as Naomi says, *"you didn't do anything wrong Maxwell."* Elsewhere, Kaiden comes out of the washroom and sees Destiny holding his glasses; Kaiden says, *"my glasses."* Destiny wipes it and hands it to him. Destiny apologizes and says, *"you didn't deserve that on your first day."*

Kaiden's top is still messy; Destiny says, *"I think I know the one place where you can get cleaned up."* Destiny brings Kaiden to the ground floor as Destiny meets the cleaner named Ms. Rosewell. Ms. Rosewell said, *"Destiny child you shouldn't be down here."* Destiny says, *"I know Annie, but can you help me, please? This is my friend Kaiden."* Ms. Rosewell sees Kaiden smelling and dirty she asks, *"why is zis handsome fella smelling coke-coke?".* Kaiden says, *"um Destiny are you sure we can be in this place?"* Ms. Rosewell looks around and then lets them in. Destiny says,

36

"*Kaiden you need to get out of your clothes.*" Kaiden goes in the back, changes and hands Destiny his glasses. Destiny picks a black shirt and gives it to Kaiden. Ms. Rosewell starts the washing machine as Kaiden comes out wearing the shirt as Destiny looks at him and thinks, '*wow he looks so handsome in the shirt.*' Kaiden says, "*Destiny?*". Destiny asks, "*sorry what is it?*". Kaiden replies, "*can I have my glasses back please?*". Destiny gives it to him as Kaiden wears it; Destiny says, "*you have beautiful eyes.*" Kaiden laughs and replies, "*thanks.*" Ms. Rosewell says, "*you two kids better head for class.*" They soon come back upstairs with Kaiden saying, "*thanks for helping me, Destiny.*" Destiny replies, "*it's ok*". As they smile at each other. Jen says, "*there you two are.*"

They head to class Maxwell says, "*babes.*" Destiny ignores him and sits with Kaiden to study in the class. Soon after college; Maxwell pulls Destiny into a classroom as Destiny said, "*Maxwell I don't want to talk to you.*" Maxwell says, "*babes please I'm sorry. I was angry.*" Destiny says, "*I have to get ready for practice.*" She leaves and comes to change into her cheerleading uniform. Jen asks, "*what happened between you and Kaiden?*". Destiny replies, "*I helped him; he didn't deserve what Maxwell did to him.*" Before Destiny can go outside; Kaiden stops her and says, "*um... Destiny?*". Destiny turns to see Kaiden who apologizes for the coffee shop incident; he then gives her a wrapped present. Destiny says, "*I can't take this.*" Kaiden says, "*you called me your friend. I want you to accept this please.*" Destiny smiles and thanks him; Kaiden says, "*don't worry Destiny your secret is safe with me.*" Destiny heads out to cheerleading practice; Naomi and her minions witness Destiny and Kaiden together as Naomi says to her minions, "*girls I think Kaiden will be a good use to our plan*".

Chapter 18

The next day at school Kaiden saw Destiny as they shared a smile. Maxwell noticed this and came over to Destiny and said, *"hey babes."* Soon, the teacher came in and the lesson started; Jen says, *"let's hope we will have a drama-free day."* Naomi smiles at Maxwell who he rolls his eyes at her. At lunch Naomi meets Michelle and Kitty in a private classroom as Naomi said, *"could you guys believe Maxwell rolled his eyes at me?"*. Michelle asked, *"is the plan still in motions?"*. Naomi laughed and nodded; in the canteen Destiny and Jen were eating as Kaiden approached them asking, *"can I sit with you?"*. Jen nods replying, *"sure."* Maxwell comes in and sees Destiny as he comes over saying, *"babes I need you to come with me."* Destiny says, *"Maxwell I am having lunch right now."* Maxwell grabs Destiny's hand and pulls her to leave. Kaiden asks, *"is he always like that to Destiny?"*. Jen nods as Naomi bumps into Maxwell who lets go of Destiny's hand. Destiny says shocked, *"Maxwell what the hell is wrong with you?"*. Naomi says, *"Maxwell we need to talk."*

Naomi signals her minions; Destiny heads back to her seat as she is about slip when Kaiden gets up and holds her. Destiny and Kaiden share an eyelock as Maxwell turns to see. Naomi says, *"Maxwell we need to talk in private."* They head out; Kaiden helps Destiny up as Jen asks, *"Destiny are you ok?"*. Destiny thanks Kaiden and leaves. Kaiden looks around the room and sees Michelle and Kitty exchanging handshakes. As they head out; Kaiden follows them and overhears Michelle and Kitty talk about the plan. Michelle says, *"it's only a matter of time before Kaiden falls in love with Destiny."* Kaiden says, *"you two."* Michelle and

Kitty turn to see Kaiden as Kaiden says *"you think it's funny to play around with someone's life? to use me in your sick twisted plan?"*. The girls try to explain themselves; Kaiden gives them a warning to not interfere or try anything else. Michelle and Kitty nod as they leave.

Maxwell and Naomi are in the corridor as Maxwell says, *"this had better be good Naomi."* Naomi says, *"Maxwell, I know you and Destiny are together."* Naomi tries to explain things and comes closer; Maxwell asks, *"what are you doing Naomi?"*. Maxwell opens the door and leaves as Naomi scowls angrily and thinks, *'I am going to make you mine Maxwell.'* Elsewhere, Jen comes outside to Destiny and gives her a drink. Destiny sighs saying, *"we couldn't go by another day without drama."* Jen says, *"you know I will always have your back Destiny."* They both share a smile as the bell rings for class; after-college Jen and Destiny prepare for cheerleading practice. Maxwell is training on the pitch and sees Destiny as they share an eyelock; Maxwell notices that Destiny's stare is cold. As Maxwell leads the team; Destiny is trying to stay focus on her team. Kaiden comes and sees the coach asking, *"coach can I try-out for the team please?"*. Maxwell and the guys look at Kaiden who has a firm smile on his face.

Chapter 19

A s Kaiden awaited the response; Maxwell laughed and says, *"how can a geek like you play football?"*. The coach says, *"Maxwell have you forgotten the rules on how to speak with everyone?"*. The coach comes to Kaiden and says, *"Kaiden you have only just joined this college."* Kaiden says, *"I understand sir, I just want one chance."* Maxwell gives Kaiden a cold look as the coach looks at his team and says, *" I know we held the cheerleading try-outs, but Kaiden looks like a promising student; therefore in a few days there will be a try-out."* As the guys were talking amongst themselves; some were worried they might lose their place whilst others were ready to give it their best. The coach leaves and dismisses the team; Maxwell sees Kaiden and says, *"a geek boy like you will never make the team."* Maxwell leaves as Destiny also tells the girls that practice is over. Jen notices Kaiden as she is about to go over; Destiny says, *"Jen I think I should sort things out."* Jen says, *"Destiny, Kaiden is my friend too."* Jen and Destiny come over asking Kaiden, *"what happened?"*. Kaiden tells them about the football try-out.

Later that evening Kaiden is in his room working out as he looks out of his window; Destiny is in her room reading a book. Destiny looks out as Kaiden is about to say something however Marie calls him. Kaiden heads downstairs as Destiny turns off her lights and goes to sleep. Kaiden heads back upstairs and looks out of his window and notices Destiny's curtains closed as he thinks, *'Destiny must have gone to sleep.'* The next day at school Maxwell gives Kaiden a cold stare as Destiny and Jen come to Kaiden. Kaiden asks, *"Destiny I have something to ask you?"*. Naomi notices the tension between Kaiden,

Maxwell, and Destiny. Michelle and Kitty come to Naomi saying, *"the plan is still going to work."* Michelle says, *"actually Kaiden found out about the plan and threatened us."* Naomi angrily says, *"what! girls you should have told me, who does he think he is?".* Naomi was about to go over and give Destiny and Kaiden a piece of her mind when she soon slips and fell on the wet floor.

Ms. Rosewell says, *"oops sorry zi floor was slippery".* Naomi says, *"you stupid cleaner? how dare you to ruin my dress and heels?".* Destiny and the student gather around as some of them laugh, take a picture as Kitty and Michelle help Naomi up. Ms. Rosewell leaves as Naomi thinks, *'don't think I have forgotten this Destiny; you will still pay'.* As the bell rings for class, Destiny sees Ms. Rosewell who says, *"do not worry over wannabe barbie. In my country zis is a punishment for her."* Destiny thanks Ms. Roswell and heads to class. The teacher says, *"welcome class; first of all, I hope your partner projects are ready for Friday".* As the teacher makes some more announcements; Kaiden watches Destiny. Maxwell notices this and thinks, *'this geek has to pay.'* At lunch, Jen and Destiny are doing some cheerleading practice training whilst Kaiden was working out in the gym when Maxwell comes with his friends. Kaiden sees Maxwell with his friends and says, *"hey Maxwell what do you want?".* Maxwell replies with a punch as his friends attack Kaiden. Maxwell beats Kaiden up and says, *"hey four-eyes if you look at my girl or even talk to her you will suffer worse."* As Kaiden coughs and lays back; he remembers a memory of when he was beaten younger.

Chapter 20

Kaiden gets up and walks toward the mirror; he sees bruises and cuts on his face. he holds his broken glasses and grabs his bag; in-class Destiny and Jen wonder, 'where's Kaiden?'. Maxwell has a smirk on his face; Destiny takes Kaiden's number from Jen. Kaiden gets first-aid from the nurse as he sees Destiny passing and hides; the nurses say, "Mr. Turner my office is not a hiding place." As Kaiden comes out; Jen sees him as Kaiden sighs. Jen asks, "what happened to your face Kaiden?". Kaiden says, "please don't tell Destiny." Later that evening Destiny comes to her favourite place in the church as Kaiden also comes to pray; Destiny thinks, 'why has Kaiden avoided me today?'. Kaiden winces as he gets up from the prayer; Destiny turns and sees Kaiden; he tries to run but falls. Destiny sees Kaiden's face and legs arms covered with bruises. She helps him up and says, "Kaiden oh my god? what happened to you?". Kaiden tries to brush her off and says, "leave me alone."

Destiny says, "stop it Kaiden. I'm not going to abandon you." Destiny notices the injuries and says, "let me drop you to the hospital." They soon arrive at the hospital; Destiny stays by Kaiden's side as the doctor does some tests and scans. The doctor advises Kaiden to get bed rest for two weeks. Kaiden has a flashback memory of when he was beaten up as a child by some bullies however a young girl had come and helped him. Kaiden sees Destiny and thinks 'why does she feel so familiar?'. Destiny says, "Kaiden you have to be honest with me. who is responsible for your state?". Kaiden is reluctant to say whilst Destiny thinks and says, "let me drop you home." She takes Kaiden down her street as Kaiden says, "I will

42

manage from here." Kaiden heads into his house, Destiny watches him and thinks, *'he's the new neighbour. wow what a small world!.'* Marie was shocked to see Kaiden's state as Kaiden says, *"I'll be fine mom."*

Soon Destiny meets Maxwell in the park; Destiny sees a roasted walnut vendor as she says, *"babes I want to see some roasted walnuts."* Maxwell leaves his jacket and goes to buy it as his phone repeatedly buzzes. Destiny takes it out as she unlocks Maxwell's phone and sees the video of Kaiden getting beaten up. Destiny is shocked saying, *"no, this can't be Maxwell he would never hurt someone else."* Maxwell comes back as Destiny says, *"Maxwell tell me this wasn't you."* Maxwell tries to avoid and change the topic however Destiny says, *" I can't believe you could hurt someone like that."* Maxwell holds his hand and says, *"babes I'm sorry I love you too much. I can't see you with anyone else".*

Destiny says, *" I think we need to go on a break."* Destiny leaves as Maxwell watches her go. Soon, his phone rings as he sees Naomi's incoming call. Naomi says, *"Maxwell come over we have to work on our project."* Maxwell left the park; Destiny came home and was about to sleep when she noticed the locket on the floor. Destiny remembered the video as she took it and locked it in a box. Destiny had tears in her eyes and wondered *'why am I crying for? who am I crying for?'.* As she slept, she saw the girl in white as Richelle says, *"you will receive happiness soon and the love which you have been longing for."* Destiny still had no idea who the person was but somehow, she managed to get some rest. The next day at college Jen sees Destiny who asks, *"are you ok?"* however Destiny ignores the question and comes to the coach's office as she knocks on the door. The coach opens the door and says, *"hi Destiny, please come in."*

Chapter 21

Destiny enters and asks, " *hi coach have you got a minute?*". The coach nods as Destiny says, *"I have something to tell you about Maxwell."* Destiny shows the video of Maxwell attacking Kaiden; the coach looks shocked and says, *"I can't believe that he would hurt a fellow pupil."* As the coach leaves the room; Destiny thinks about what she did and thinks, *'it's better this way.'* The coach announces an emergency soccer practice session as all the football players come to the field. The coach says, *"you all must be wondering why I have called you here?"*. As the players talk amongst themselves; Maxwell comes and apologizes for being late. The coach says, *"Maxwell I have received disturbing news and I have made a decision to remove you as captain and from the team."* Maxwell says, *"coach, I am your strongest player"*. As the team talk amongst themselves, the coach says, *"my decision is final."* Maxwell gets angry and says, *"who dared to go against me!"*. Destiny is in the corridor as she sees Maxwell coming up to her; however, Naomi stops Maxwell as Destiny turns and heads in the other direction. Destiny hides against the wall, however soon she feels a tap on the shoulder which scares her. She turns and says, *"Jen, you scared me."* Jen says, *"what's up? why did Coach call a meeting?"*. Destiny says, *"not here, let's talk in the canteen."* They head into the canteen as Jen is shocked after hearing that Maxwell is responsible for Kaiden's injuries.

Destiny says, *"he needed to be taught a lesson."* Jen asks, *"are you two finally broken up?"*. Destiny shakes her head and replies, *"we are on a break."* Jen rolls her eyes and says, *"I think I am going to check on Kaiden later on."* Destiny and Jen talk; Maxwell comes into the canteen and sees Destiny. Maxwell's eyes are filled with anger as he comes to Destiny and says, *"I cannot believe you told the coach about Kaiden."* Destiny says, *"you deserve the punishment, Maxwell. you cheated and felt threatened by Kaiden."* Maxwell grabs Destiny's hand to pull her out as Jen pushes him to the floor. Destiny looks at Jen and says, *"you became superwoman."* Jen laughs as Naomi comes with her friends. Maxwell gets up and says, *"you'll pay for this!".* Later that afternoon after college, Destiny came home and made chicken and pumpkin soup. A few moments later, Isabelle came home; Destiny asks, *"mom taste this please."* Isabelle says, *"yum this is delicious."* Destiny packs it and heads over to Kaiden's place. She rings the bell; Marie opens and sees Destiny. Destiny says, *"hello I am here to see Kaiden, I am Destiny, Kaiden's friend from college."* Marie smiles as she lets Destiny in and says, *"something smells delicious."*

Destiny puts the soup on the table she asks, *"where's Kaiden?".* Marie answers, *"he's upstairs."* Destiny heads upstairs, she is surprised to see Jen and Kaiden laughing as Jen says, *"hey Destiny."* Kaiden smiles at her as he says, *" it's nice of you both to come and see me."* Jen says, *"it's getting late, and I should go.";* Destiny stays by Kaiden's side and tells him, *"Kaiden I told the coach about the attack and Maxwell has been punished."* Kaiden thanks Destiny who smiles at him. Meanwhile, at Naomi's place she was waiting for Maxwell as the doorbell rang. Naomi checked herself in the mirror and opened the door to see Maxwell. Maxwell says, *"Naomi we need a plan."* Elsewhere, Marie came up with the soup as Destiny says, *"I'll see you tomorrow."* Destiny left, Marie fed Kaiden the soup; he says, *"mom this soup is delicious."* Marie replies, *"this soup was made by Destiny."* Kaiden smiles as he thinks of Destiny.

Chapter 22

M axwell says, *"I lost my place on the football team and my captaincy."* Naomi says, *"Destiny is determined to ruin everyone's life."* Maxwell asks for a drink; Naomi brings two glasses and a bottle of red wine. Maxwell says, *"you look hot".* Naomi blushes as she pours the drink; however, Maxwell passes out on the couch. Naomi covers him with a blanket and kisses his forehead; The next day Maxwell awakes with a hangover as Naomi comes downstairs and says, *"you were wasted last night."* Naomi says, *"come on Maxwell, I will give you a lift to college."* Destiny and Jen walked as Maxwell was with Naomi in her car. Destiny saw them coming in together. Jen says, *"Destiny don't worry."* In class Destiny ignores Maxwell despite his attempts to try and speak with her; meanwhile, Isabelle comes over to speak with Marie and says, *" I heard my daughter came here last night."* Kaiden comes downstairs. Isabelle notices his injuries however Marie says, *"my son is a strong fighter."* Isabelle invites Marie for a coffee who replies, *"I need to focus on Kaiden right now."* Kaiden says, *"it's ok mom you go, I will be fine."*

   In class the teacher was teaching however Destiny wasn't focused as she didn't know why but she wanted to be with Kaiden. Jen texted Kaiden as he replied, Destiny watched Jen and asked, *"who are you texting?".* Jen replies, *"Kaiden."* Destiny didn't know why but she felt a little jealous and wondered, *'does Jen like Kaiden?'.* Soon, Destiny walked down the corridor, Maxwell noticed her as Ms Rosewell was mopping the floor. Maxwell slips as Ms Rosewell says *"ze floor is slippery ja?".* Naomi helps Maxwell up; however, Ms Rosewell is shouted at by Naomi who says, *"foolish cleaner can't you do a proper job instead of hurting others?"*. Destiny takes a stand for Ms Rosewell with Naomi saying, *"you still have to pay Destiny."* Later that afternoon Destiny came to see Kaiden and began to work on their project.

Kaiden watches Destiny as he opens the window, and a small breeze blows Destiny's golden hair however the wind gets stronger; Kaiden closes the window however he is about to slip on a book. Destiny falls on the bed as Kaiden accidentally kisses her. Destiny is stunned as she looks wide-eyed at Kaiden who gets off her and says, *" I am sorry Destiny."* Destiny says, *"it's ok."* Meanwhile, Jen was at cheerleading practice and called Destiny who didn't answer. She wondered, *'where did she disappear to?'*. Destiny completes the project as Kaiden takes rest; Destiny says, *" I hope you will be able to come back soon."* As Destiny goes, she can't help but notice a photo frame on the wall.

Kaiden sleeps and remembers a little girl playing with him in the park. Kaiden thinks, *'I keep seeing this little girl in my dream. Who is she?'*. Richelle comes into Kaiden's dream and says, *"she is your true soulmate, and she is close to you."* Kaiden soon falls asleep; Destiny also sleeps in her room wondering about the kiss.

Chapter 23

The next few days passed with Kaiden fully recovered and Destiny coming to the church. Destiny confessed about her kiss as the priest says, *"child you have nothing be ashamed of."* Destiny says, *"sorry father I thought I was alone."* The priest gave some wise words to Destiny who she smiled and thanked him as she left. Meanwhile, Naomi was with her friends discussing a plan when her phone rang, she saw Maxwell's incoming call. Naomi says, *"girls I will take this phone call and be right back."* Naomi comes outside, she speaks with Maxwell and says, *" I think I know a way for me to get back with Destiny."* Naomi rolls her eyes as Maxwell speaks however Naomi says, *"I am not going let you use me to get back with your girlfriend."* Naomi disconnects the call with Maxwell who wonders, *'how will I get Destiny back?'.* The next day at college, the teacher says, *"I hope everyone has done their paired presentation as we will now be presenting it."*

Kaiden came into the class and sees Destiny who doesn't look at him. The teacher sees Kaiden and says, *"Mr. Turner I hope you are feeling well and back to study."* Kaiden nods and gets to his seat, The class begins, one by one everyone presents as Destiny and Kaiden are last to present. Destiny does very well, and everyone applauds her. Kaiden smiles and thinks, *'she's amazing.* After class Kaiden tries to speak to Destiny however Destiny heads down the corridor and says, *"Jen I need to go to the toilet."* Jen says, *"I will be waiting with Kaiden."* Maxwell comes to Kaiden and hugs him. Jen looks surprised as Maxwell says, *"it's great to see you back so soon Kaiden."* Kaiden asks *"what do you want Maxwell?".* Maxwell apologizes however Kaiden doesn't buy it and says,

"Maxwell please leave me alone." Jen and Kaiden walk away; Maxwell rolls his eyes as Naomi pulls his arm into an empty classroom asking, *"what the hell are you playing at?"*.

Maxwell replies, *"what do you care Naomi? It's not like you are going to help me."* Naomi rolls her eyes and says, *"fine I will help you on one condition."* Destiny walks down the corridor; Naomi pulls Maxwell closer. Destiny sees Naomi hugging Maxwell. As Destiny walks off; Naomi smirks as Maxwell says, *"why did you hug me? what's your condition?"*. Naomi says, *"whatever I say goes."* Destiny comes to the canteen and sees Jen and Kaiden talking. Kaiden sees her as Jen turns and says, *"Destiny you took so long."* Destiny comes over and sits; Kaiden smiles at her as Jen says, *"I will get you some chips."* Destiny tries to avoid eye-contact with Kaiden as he says, *" it's ok, you don't have to be embarrassed because we kissed."* Destiny was nervous as she says *"Kaiden I don't think what we have is..."*; just then Maxwell came in holding Naomi's hand. Destiny was stunned as Maxwell kisses Naomi's cheek. Destiny gets up and runs out; Kaiden goes after her to find her upset. Destiny says, *"I am not crying."* Kaiden places a hand on her shoulder as she says, *"please leave me alone Kaiden."* Kaiden says *"I am not going to abandon my friend."*

Chapter 24

Kaiden comforts Destiny as Jen comes holding the chips and sees Destiny upset. Jen passes the chips to Kaiden. Destiny and Jen hug as Jen says, *"we are going to talk about this."* Destiny says, *"Jen we don't need to."* Jen takes the chips and says, *"come on Destiny."* Kaiden heads back to the canteen, sees Maxwell with his friends and marches up to him. Kaiden says, *"you hurt Destiny."* Maxwell rolls his eyes as he pushes Kaiden and says, *"what does it bother you? stay out of my business geek."* Meanwhile, Destiny and Jen are sitting on the bench under the tree, Jen wipes Destiny's tears and says, *"I can't believe Maxwell, he was holding hands with Naomi."* Jen says, *"he doesn't deserve you."* Kaiden is on his way to see Destiny when he bumps into the coach who says, *"Ah Kaiden what a delight you have come back, please follow me."* The coach takes Kaiden with him and talks the whole way. Jen says, *"I have just thing to cheer you up today."* Soon, the bell rings, Destiny, and Jen head to class as Maxwell looks at Destiny and then Naomi. Kaiden comes in; Destiny smiles and the class begins. Destiny says, *"thanks for trying to cheer me up."* Kaiden smiles as she says, *"and you know about the kiss..."*; Kaiden acts awkwardly as Destiny laughs and says, *"it was accidental, and I was just being stupid. let's just forget about it."*

Later that afternoon; Jen and Destiny were practicing cheerleading as the soccer team came onto the pitch; Kaiden came out wearing his kit as all the girls began to swoon over him. The coach came on the pitch and said, *"Kaiden I want you to lead this practice and train the team up."* Kaiden felt a little nervous however as he looked at the cheerleading squad; Jen and Destiny gave him a reassuring smile. Just as Kaiden was about to start practice; Maxwell came on the pitch. The coach said, "*Maxwell what are you doing here?*". Maxwell says, "*Coach, you wanted to have a trial to see who's the best captain for the team and I want to have the trial with Kaiden.*" The coach said firmly, "*I have already made my decision.*" Maxwell held a book and read, '*page 45 of the school sports page indicates that the captain cannot be removed without the consent of its player and if a new captain is to take place there must be a fair trial'*. As the soccer team players speak amongst themselves; Kaiden gives Maxwell a cold stare.

Naomi comes over with Kitty and Michelle; she smirks at Destiny as Jen says, "*what do you want?*". Naomi replies, "*aww little sidekick of Destiny, there's so much I want but I don't need to tell you.*" Kitty and Michelle laugh, Jen says, "*I am Destiny's best friend which means more than being a sidekick or minion.*" Destiny asks, "*Naomi what do you want?*". Naomi drops to Destiny's feet and begs to let back on the team. The coach comes over; Naomi fakes her tears and says, "*I want a chance coach to be back on the team.*" Jen rolls her eyes and says, "*nope we don't need her on the team.*" Coach says, "*come to the pitch.*" As the cheerleading squad come over, Kaiden and Destiny look at each other as everyone talks and the coach blows a whistle and says, " *practice is cancelled for today but Maxwell, Destiny, Jen, Kaiden and Naomi please stay behind.*" Everyone leaves, the principal comes to the pitch as Maxwell says, "*sir right on time.*" The principal has a private chat with the coach who soon comes back and says, "*Kaiden and Maxwell will have a match between them for tomorrow to see who is better to be captain.*" Destiny is stunned and protests, "*Coach you cannot allow this, you saw what he did to Kaiden.*" Naomi says, "*what about my place on the cheerleading squad coach?*". The coach apologizes and leaves as Naomi scowls at Jen who laughs at her.

Chapter 25

The next day, the coach spoke with the players as he divided the team in half; Maxwell had half of the players as did Kaiden. The coach said, "*you each will be responsible for training your team and the match will be later this afternoon.*" Maxwell says, "*ok team, let's begin.*" Maxwell gives Kaiden a cold stare as he leaves to start training; Kaiden says, "*ok guys let's begin with warm-ups.*". Destiny and Jen see Maxwell and Kaiden training their team; Jen says, "*I am sure Kaiden will win the match this afternoon.*" Naomi comes and says, "*as if.*" She pushes past Destiny. Destiny says, "*Jen let's just focus on giving Kaiden the support.*" The morning training finishes as the college has been given a half-day to watch the match in the afternoon; the principal starts with a speech and says, "*may the best man win.*" Destiny and Jen cheer for Kaiden, Naomi comes with her minions and begins to cheer for Maxwell. Naomi looks at Destiny asking, " *won't you support your boyfriend?*". Destiny replies, "*my relationship to Kaiden is none of your business.*" As the crowd cheer, the coach blows the whistle as the game begins.

Destiny, Jen, and the cheerleaders chant, '*KAIDEN*'; Kaiden sees Destiny and smiles but then focuses on the game; Maxwell notices Kaiden is doing well as he sees his friend on the other team and gives him a nod. Kaiden gets the ball as Maxwell's friend takes it and passes it to Maxwell however before Maxwell can shoot; Kaiden steals the ball back. Destiny says "*Kaiden is so good at soccer.*" Naomi chants, '*GO MAXWELL*'. Maxwell sees Kaiden is about to score and trips him; the coach notices this and says, "*foul.*" Maxwell says, "*coach come on.*" Kaiden gets back up as he takes a break with his team to replan their strategies. Maxwell says, *"we've got to beat them and be tougher."* The principal says, *"nothing like a bit of competition to boost the college team spirit."* Jen says *"Destiny, I need to go to the toilet."* Destiny nods and says, *"ok"*. As the second half begins of the match; Kaiden and Maxwell seem to both have strength; Kaiden manages to score a goal for his team. As the crowd cheers, Maxwell gets angry seeing Kaiden smiling as Destiny who cheers for him. Maxwell runs off to the bleachers and speaks with Naomi and says, *"I need you to do something."* Maxwell whispers her something; Naomi smiles and replies, *"perfect."*

The coach comes on the field and says, "*Kaiden has scored one goal; Maxwell is yet to score."* Naomi speaks to her minions and gives them instructions. They both leave, As Kaiden's and Maxwell's match recommences; Destiny is cheering with the girls and soon wonders, *'what's taking Jen so long?'.* Elsewhere, Jen washes her hand and opens the door however she is shocked to find it is locked. Jen bangs on the door and says, *"HELLO?? ANYONE THERE???".* Maxwell soon manages to score a goal; leaving the scores to be tied. Destiny gets down from the bleachers; Naomi spots her and comes after her; Naomi grabs Destiny's arm and brings her to the high-top stand; Destiny says, *"Naomi what the hell? let me go."* Naomi pushes Destiny who screams as Kaiden sees her falling. He runs towards her as Destiny closes her eyes however soon she feels that someone has saved her. Maxwell scores the goal and cheers. Destiny opens her eyes as she is stunned to see Kaiden holding her; Kaiden asks, *"are you ok?".* Meanwhile, the cleaner opens the toilets as Jen grabs her bag and runs. Kaiden places Destiny on the ground as everyone begins to gather around her.

Chapter 26

Jen came running back into the field; everyone was around Destiny; Kaiden got brought her some water. Kaiden helps Destiny up as the coach asks, *"what happened? how did you fall from there?".* Destiny looks at Naomi and replies, *"she pushed me."* Naomi says, *"how dare you to accuse me of such a thing?".* Jen sees Destiny and asks, *"what happened?".* The coach speaks with the principal as everyone comes back to their places and wait for the results. Maxwell has a smug smile on his face as Kaiden stands with the players, who say, *"even if you don't make captain, you were the best."* Maxwell rolls his eyes as the coach says, *"I want to announce that despite everything, someone showed true loyalty and sportsmanship in this match."* The coach says, *"I am pleased to announce the captain of the football team will be...".* Everyone waits in anticipation; Maxwell comes over to shake the coach's hand. However, he ignores Maxwell and comes to Kaiden to shake his hand saying, *"Kaiden congratulation, you are the new captain of the team."* Destiny, Jen, and everyone applauds and cheer for him as Maxwell leaves in anger. The team lift Kaiden who smiles happily. Later after college that afternoon, Jen treats Destiny and Kaiden to a milkshake as they talk about the day. Kaiden says, *"I can't believe I am the new captain."* Destiny raises the milkshake and says, *"well deserve and to our new friend captain Kaiden."* They take a selfie; Destiny comes to the counter to order ice cream, just then Maxwell enters and sees Destiny. Maxwell comes and hugs Destiny saying, *"babes I was so worried."*

Destiny pushes Maxwell and says, *"what the hell?".* Maxwell tries to act sorry as Kaiden comes over and says, *"Destiny are you ok?".* Destiny nods as Maxwell say, "*so Mr. Captain, celebrating your pity victory?*". Destiny looks at Maxwell saying, "*why are you acting like this?*". Maxwell replies, "*he's stolen my captaincy and now you are defending him.*" Destiny says, "*you are acting like a complete jerk.*" Maxwell rolls his eyes and leaves. Destiny heads back to finish her milkshake. Maxwell comes to meet Naomi who says, "*I think Kaiden has a soft spot for Destiny.*" As Maxwell is in thought, Naomi comes and sits closer to Maxwell as she kisses him. Maxwell pushes Naomi off and stands up shocked asking, " *Naomi what did you do that?*". Naomi replies, "*remember our deal.*" Naomi comes closer to Maxwell; she pulls him closer and kisses him. Maxwell thinks, '*wow she is actually a good kisser.*' On their way home, Kaiden and Destiny talk with each other as Destiny feels hurt by Maxwell's behaviour. Kaiden says, "*you deserve to be treated like a princess.*" Destiny smiles and says, "*thanks Kaiden.*" Destiny comes home and is surprised to see Marie waiting for her. Destiny says, "*hi, is everything ok?*". Isabelle enters the room as Marie gets up and hugs Destiny. Destiny wonders, '*has something happened?*'.

Chapter 27

Marie says, *"I was waiting for you to come back. Actually, I know you and my son are good friends and I was wondering if you would like to join us for dinner one day."* Destiny smiled and said, *"we are just friends, and it seems like you think I could be his girlfriend."* Marie soon leaves as Isabelle notices Destiny is about to tell her something. Destiny says *"mom, things between me and Maxwell right now are complicated."* Destiny heads upstairs, showers and get some rest. Meanwhile, Maxwell leaves Naomi's place and is in deep thoughts. Marie comes home; Kaiden asks, *"mom where were you?".* Marie replies, *"just at the neighbour's."* The next day at college, Naomi is holding Maxwell's hand as Destiny sees them together. She feels a small pain in her heart. Jen comes over to her saying, *"don't think about them. I am sure you will find someone even more amazing soon."* The bell rings for class, Kaiden comes on his way as Maxwell's friend ambush him and smash his glasses. Mrs. Rosewell notices Kaiden's state and says, *"you need to make ze stand."* Kaiden came into class; the girls noticed Kaiden looked sexier and handsome without his glasses. Destiny looked at Kaiden, they both shared a smile. Soon classes finished for the afternoon; Kaiden was on his way to the gym when Destiny calls out, *"Kaiden hold on."*

Destiny says, *"Mrs. Rosewell told me what happened today, and I want to help you."* Kaiden asks, *"how?".* Destiny brings him to the mall; she helps him change his style and also takes Kaiden to the opticians. As Kaiden tries contact lenses; Destiny gives him a thumbs up asking, *"what do you think?".* Kaiden looks in the mirror and smiles. They soon head to have afternoon tea; Destiny can't help think of her relationship with Maxwell. Kaiden notices Destiny is sad and tries to cheer her up by dancing and singing for her. Destiny laughs and says, *"you're funny Kaiden."* They soon head home. Maxwell sees Destiny and Kaiden close wondering, *'is there something going on between the two of them?'*. As Kaiden comes into his house, Destiny crosses the road and sees Maxwell waiting for her on the doorstep. Destiny asks, *"Maxwell what are you doing here?"*. Maxwell replies, *"we need to talk."* They talk with Maxwell telling Destiny, *"I miss you."* Maxwell begs for another chance. Destiny thinks about their relationship and nods as Maxwell happily hugs Destiny.

Over the next few days at college, Maxwell hangs out with Destiny and tries to work their relationship out. Naomi scowls watching them together as Maxwell comes to the washroom; Naomi ambushes him and says, *"so you're back with your ex?"*. Naomi says, *"I thought we had something special."* Naomi kisses Maxwell who pushes her against the wall; Naomi wraps her legs around Maxwell. Meanwhile, Destiny is in the library as Jen soon comes over to her. Jen says, *"I feel like I haven't seen you in forever bestie."* Destiny says, *"yeah I've been busy."* Jen says, *"so you're back with Maxwell."* Destiny nods and says, *"yeah I wanted to give us another chance."* Elsewhere, Maxwell comes out of the washroom checking himself; Naomi thinks, *'now I know that me and Maxwell have a connection, I just need to get rid of Destiny and make him mine forever.'* Kaiden walked down the corridor as Naomi came out of the washroom. She was looking messy and noticed Kaiden saying, *"wow, you look yummy"*. Kaiden rolls his eyes answering, *"dream on Naomi, I'm not going to fall for your tricks."*

Chapter 28

Kaiden comes to the library and sees Destiny. He tries to come over to talk when Maxwell comes and holds Destiny close saying, *"babes I missed you."* They share a kiss as Maxwell looks at Kaiden saying, *"hey, Kaiden bro, no hard feelings over the captaincy of the soccer team".* At practice after college, Maxwell was with Destiny trying to romance however she brushes him off and says, *"I need to get to cheerleading practice."* Destiny leaves, Maxwell rolls his eyes and calls Naomi; Jen sees Destiny coming asking, *"where were you?".* Destiny and Jen begin practice as Kaiden trains the team-up. After the practice, Kaiden sees Destiny and asks, *"wanna go watch a movie?".* Jen notices Kaiden looking at Destiny intensely. Destiny smiles and replies, *"sure."* Destiny heads to get change, Jen stops Kaiden and says, *"I know you have feelings for Destiny."* Kaiden says, *"what? that's crazy we are just friends."* Kaiden heads to get change leaving Jen in thoughts. Meanwhile, Naomi is at her house watching a movie as the doorbell rings and she opens to see Maxwell. Maxwell is holding a bottle of champagne; Naomi invites him in. Naomi gets the glasses and asks, *"Maxwell what are we celebrating?".* Maxwell replies, *"well I am back with Destiny."* Naomi gets angry with Maxwell and throws a pillow at him yelling, *" GET OUT MAXWELL."*

Maxwell comes closer to Naomi saying, *"I know you don't mean that."* Naomi feels herself falling for Maxwell's charms. Maxwell pulls her close and says, *"even if I am back with Destiny that doesn't mean the end of us."* Naomi coldly says, *" I am nobody seconds."* Maxwell touches Naomi, she closes her eyes with Maxwell saying, *"what we have is special and I don't want anyone to come between us, I want you."* Naomi opens her eyes and looks at Maxwell as she takes his hand, and they head upstairs. Meanwhile, Kaiden and Destiny were at the cinema; there were so many great movies showing. Kaiden and Destiny couldn't decide what to watch, Kaiden asks, *"how about we toss a coin for it?".* Destiny nods as he flips a coin. Kaiden sees he has won however says, *"Destiny you choose."* Destiny replies, *"I choose West Side Story."* They soon get into the screening room, Kaiden says, *"I thought you would have chosen, no time to die".* Destiny shakes her head saying, *"it's a sad movie and I will need more tissues and ice cream."* Kaiden smiles at her. The movie soon begins however Kaiden can't help but watch Destiny and thinks, *'she's so amazing I wish she wasn't with Maxwell.'* Destiny watches the movie and puts her hand in the popcorn. She feels Kaiden's hand and looks at him. Kaiden looks back at the screen leaving Destiny to wonder, *'why does Kaiden's touch feel so familiar?'.*

Later that evening Kaiden and Destiny walk on the way home; Destiny asks Kaiden about Soccer. Kaiden says, *"I've always loved sports, particularly soccer."* Kaiden drops Destiny home and thanks him for the movie. Kaiden says, *"Destiny you know there's a rule in friendship".* Destiny was confused as Kaiden smiles and says, *"no sorry and no thank you."* Kaiden says, *"I'll see you at college tomorrow."* As Kaiden comes home, he climbs the stairs, opens his room, and sees the framed photo of the girl and says, *"wherever you are now I know that I will find you soon."* The next morning early, Naomi's phone rings as she turns to see it is Kitty. Naomi turns and sees Maxwell sleeping beside her. She blushes remembering their love last night. Naomi gets up, comes into the shower however someone comes behind her and says, *"it's not nice you left me alone in bed."* Naomi turns as Maxwell pins her arms on the wall. Naomi says, *"Maxwell, you scared me."* Maxwell says, *"I guess you need to get punished for leaving me."* He kisses her passionately as she wraps her arms around him, he lifts her in his arm as the hot water pours on them. After a long hot sexy shower, Naomi changes as Maxwell leaves, Naomi calls Kitty to meet up.

Chapter 29

Destiny meets Kaiden on the way to college, Jen comes asking, *"how was the movie last night? what did you watch?"*. Destiny replies, *"West Side Story."* Jen is surprised and says, *"no way I thought you would have watched no Time to Die"*. They soon head to class however the coach stops them. They are called into the office, at first they wonder, *'why have we been called in? are we in trouble?'*. The coach says, *"the college will be soon holding their first match against Lakers."* Kaiden says, *"you mean Lakers District College?"*. The coach nods and says, *"I need all three of you to be at your best."* As the bell's rings for class, the coach says, *"Jen you may go, I will speak with Destiny and Kaiden."* Jen leaves as the coach says, *"further to the upcoming match, I have arranged for next weekend for a small camping trip to help the team bond."* Destiny says, *"coach I will have to think about this."* Kaiden agrees as the coach says, *" of course no rush"*. In class Jen was waiting for her friends who then arrives. Destiny says, *"I will explain after class."* Naomi came in with her minions, she had an evil sly smirk on her face as Destiny says, *"the award for the smirkiest cow goes to Nomi."* The class laugh at Naomi who says, *"Destiny you brat!"*. Maxwell comes in and sits with Naomi. The teacher soon comes in as the class begins. Elsewhere, Marie is doing some shopping as she bumps into Isabelle; they starts talking about their kids. Marie says, *"I feel that Kaiden has changed so much since we moved here."* Isabelle says, *" my Destiny must be taking good care of him."* Meanwhile, back in college, Kaiden walks down the corridor when he accidentally bumps into Maxwell. Maxwell says, *"watch where you are going freak! even if you changed your style, you will always be a geek."*

Maxwell pushes him to the floor as Jen runs over and says, " *Maxwell how could you do that to Kaiden?* ". Destiny comes over to her friends as Maxwell walks away; Kaiden wipes a tear from his eyes. Destiny felt sad for Kaiden and said, "*Kaiden I have a surprise for you after school.*"

Elsewhere, Maxwell meets Naomi in the janitor's closet who says, "*Maxwell I don't want to be in such a filthy room.*" Maxwell pulls her close and says, "*we can make love wherever we want and babes this relationship is secretly discreet.*" Naomi kisses Maxwell as she says, "*you are wearing too many clothes.*" They become more passionate and remove each other's clothes whilst Naomi moans Maxwell's name. Maxwell kisses Naomi's neck however a knock on the door interrupts them. Mrs. Rosewell says, "*hello is there anyone inside?*". Naomi and Maxwell look around, grabbing their clothes and hide in another closet. Mrs. Rosewell opens the door and puts the light on. She looks around and says, "*I could have thought I heard ze noises coming through ere.*" She locks the door as Maxwell, and Naomi both sigh with relief. Naomi gets dressed and says, "*Maxwell that was close.*" Maxwell puts his pants on and pulls Naomi closer. Naomi says, "*it's too dangerous here, and what if anyone finds out?*". Maxwell says, "*no one will find out my sexy doll.*" Naomi heads out with Maxwell coming after her.

After college, Destiny brings Kaiden to the church as they both pray. The priest comes and notices Kaiden has a lot on his mind. The priest says, "*why don't you go into the confession?*". Destiny says to Kaiden, " *I will wait for you outside.*" Kaiden goes into the booth and tells everything including his feelings for Destiny. Destiny awaits outside however gets a call from Maxwell and ignores it. Jen calls Destiny and asks to meet up. Kaiden comes outside; Destiny asks, "*how are you feeling Kaiden?*". Kaiden replies, "*better thanks.*" Destiny says, "*Jen is waiting for us at the dessert parlour.*" They soon head over and order their desserts. Kaiden and Destiny tell Jen about the camping trip. Jen and Kaiden are excited as Destiny says, " *it will be amazing but first I need to talk to Maxwell about it.*" Soon their sundaes arrive,

Kaiden looked at Destiny and says, *"you are your own person."* Destiny says, *"yeah but Maxwell is my boyfriend."* Jen rolls her eyes and says, *"I wish you would just dump him; he doesn't deserve you."* Destiny felt annoyed, got up and left.

Chapter 30

The next day Kaiden gets dressed and comes downstairs. Marie looks at him with tears in her eyes asking, *"where is my handsome son off to?"*. Kaiden replies, *"mom please don't get emotional."* The doorbell rings as Kaiden opens to see Destiny who says, *"I thought we could go to college together."* They leave and head together. Soon in class all the girls fawn over Kaiden with Destiny and Jen being the only ones who seem normal. Maxwell comes and sees Destiny saying, *"I feel like we haven't seen each other in a few days. let's hang out at the break."* Destiny nods: Naomi comes in as Maxwell gives Naomi a sly wink. Naomi blushes as Kitty notices this, at break Destiny and Maxwell are outside. Maxwell smokes as Destiny says, *"I thought you stopped smoking."* Maxwell puffs and says, *"come on babes."* Kaiden sees Destiny coughing over the smoke and comes over pulling Destiny's hand and says, *"Maxwell you shouldn't be smoking around Destiny like this."* Maxwell says, *"listen Kaiden, Destiny is my girl, and I can do whatever I want."* Destiny gets annoyed with Maxwell and heads over to the library. As Naomi sees Maxwell. Kitty calls out to her and says, *"something is going between you and Maxwell."* Naomi tries to deny it, Kitty says, *"maybe I should go and talk to Maxwell."* Naomi pulls Kitty back and says, *"don't ok! me and Maxwell have been..."* Kitty is stunned and shocked by what she hears. Naomi says, *"you have to promise to not tell anyone."* She nods as Naomi watches Maxwell smoking.

In the library, Destiny is annoyed with Maxwell as Kaiden comes there. Destiny says *"Kaiden you helped me out."* Kaiden smiles and says, *" what are friends for?"*. Destiny heads over to grab a book however notices it is high up, she climbs the ladder as Kaiden watches her; however, she suddenly feels the step is slippery and is about to fall when Kaiden catches her. Destiny opens her eyes and looks at Kaiden remembering when he first held her. Destiny wonders, '*am I developing feelings for Kaiden?.*' Naomi comes into the library, she spots Kaiden, and Destiny sharing a romantic moment and takes a picture thinking, '*I think Maxwell will have a lot to say for this photo.*' After school at practice the coach addresses the cheerleading squad and the soccer team about the next week upcoming camping trip. Later that evening as Naomi comes to Maxwell's place as he opens the door and says, "*sexy doll what a surprise!*". Naomi looks at Maxwell's room as Maxwell says, "*would you like a drink or anything?*". Naomi shows Maxwell's the photo of Destiny and Kaiden; Maxwell feels anger. Just as he is about to leave Naomi pulls his hand and holds him saying, "*why are you still with Destiny? I can give you so much more.*" She kisses him passionately; they fall onto Maxwell's bed as Maxwell removes his shirt. Naomi says, "*I don't think I will ever get tired of seeing your abs.*" They both kiss passionately, the doorbell rings as Destiny knocks on the door and says, "*Maxwell are you in?*".

Maxwell says, "*Destiny?*". He gets up and says, "*Naomi you need to hide.*" As Maxwell pushes her into the closet and grabs her clothes she scowls angrily. Maxwell opens the door to see Destiny outside and invites her. Maxwell says, "*sorry I was in the shower.*" Destiny says," *Maxwell I have something to tell you.*" Destiny tells Maxwell about the camping trip for next weekend. Maxwell says, "*of course you should go babes.*" Maxwell was about to kiss Destiny who says, "*I need to go but thanks for agreeing to the trip.*" After leaving Maxwell sits on his bed as Naomi angrily bangs on the door. Maxwell opens and says, "*sexy doll.*" Naomi felt annoyed grabbing her shoes and left. Maxwell calls out to her as Naomi opens the door and slams it in anger. Elsewhere, Destiny walked home, she remembered turning away when Maxwell tried to kiss her and is lost in deep thoughts. She sees Kaiden sitting on her doorstep as Kaiden says, *"hey Destiny I wanted to know if you wanted to get a milkshake."* Destiny nodded and they headed to the dessert parlour. Destiny talked about her feelings and Kaiden asked, *"do you love Maxwell?"*. Destiny didn't know how to reply whilst Kaiden thought, *'I wish she would be honest about her feelings.'* Soon it begins to get late as Destiny and Kaiden each go home to sleep. Later that night Destiny has a dream in which Maxwell is dancing with her as they are about to kiss; suddenly Destiny finds herself in a dreamworld as Richelle says, *"you gave the loser another chance?"*. Destiny was confused and says, *"loser? what are you talking about and who are you?"*. Richelle says, *"well I hope that you will be able to change your fate in time."* Richelle disappears as Destiny awakes, looks around and then falls back to sleep.

Chapter 31

The next day Destiny comes to school without Kaiden as she thought about her dream and Kaiden's words for last night, *'do you love Maxwell?'.* Jen ran and came to Destiny and says, *"hey didn't you hear me calling you?".* Destiny apologizes as Jen said, *"I am so excited for the trip next weekend."* As Destiny came into class, she looked for Maxwell. Meanwhile, Naomi walked down the corridor annoyed when someone grabbed her arm and pulled her into an empty classroom and locked the door. Naomi turned to see Maxwell as Naomi looked at him angrily and says, *"Maxwell what the hell! let me out."* Naomi reaches to try and open the door however Maxwell grabs her waist and spins her as Naomi says, *"Maxwell leave me alone, I have nothing to talk to you about."* Maxwell apologies whilst Naomi says, *"I don't want to hear your fake apologies."* Maxwell's phone rings and he lets Naomi go who coldly says, *"It's probably your beloved girlfriend."* Maxwell ignores the call, grabs Naomi, and says, *"look at me I love you, sexy doll."* Naomi kicks Maxwell as she opens the door and runs out.

Maxwell comes into class and sees Destiny who says, *"hey babes where were you?".* Maxwell says, *"just busy."* Naomi gave Maxwell a cold stare as she turned to the front just as Kaiden came in. Destiny came and sat with Maxwell, she holds his hand and says, *"babes we should do something later, maybe lunch."* Maxwell looks at Naomi, he then kisses Destiny's cheek and says, *"anything you want babes."* Naomi felt annoyed and thought, *'I knew it, Maxwell is such a douche.'* After class Maxwell says, *"babes I have something to sort out."* Destiny felt sad as Jen says, *"you can eat lunch with me and Kaiden."* Naomi was speaking with Kitty; she felt mad about Maxwell and says *"I will be back in a sec."* As Naomi came to the vending machine to buy a drink. She felt someone's presence behind her before Naomi can pick up her drink, Maxwell grabs it. Naomi says, *"Maxwell give me back my drink."* As Maxwell runs down the corridor, Naomi comes after him as Maxwell turns into the photocopier room. Naomi turns and walks down and thinks, *'where did Maxwell go?'*. Maxwell grabs Naomi into the room and locks the door. Naomi says, *"what the hell? how dare you lock me up again?"*. The principal's secretary passes as Maxwell sees her and pushes Naomi against the wall and kisses her passionately. Naomi pulls Maxwell closer to her.

The secretary tries to open the door and says, *"I should go and let the principal know."* Maxwell kisses Naomi's neck as she says, *"Maxwell please stop playing with my feelings."* Maxwell says, *"I love you; sexy doll, and I want us to be together."* Naomi says, *"I've already told you; I am nobody's second choice."* Maxwell takes Naomi's hand and says, *"you're my drug and I need you."* Naomi rolls her eyes, grabs the drink from Maxwell's hand and opens it to drink it. Maxwell pushes her against the wall and kisses her passionately. Naomi looks stunned at him as he winks at her and she pushes him. Maxwell says, *"I love to tease you; sexy doll, your lips were so sweet."* Maxwell says, *" I will prove my love for you."* Naomi soon opens the door and leaves as Maxwell comes out. The secretary comes with the principal to open the door as she opens it, the principal says *"this room is always opened during school hours. Please don't waste my time again."* At lunch, Kaiden and Jen were talking about a Netflix show whilst Destiny was lost in thoughts. Jen waved her hand and said, *"earth to Destiny."* Destiny says, *"hey what's up?"*. Jen says, *"we were talking about squid game challenges"*. Destiny says, *"yeah it's an amazing show."* Jen and Kaiden were both worried about Destiny who got up and left.

Chapter 32

Destiny came to the library and opened the door; however, was stunned to find it was locked. As she looked up and saw, '*The library will be closed for a few hours.*' Back in the canteen Jen and Kaiden were both talking about Destiny who soon came back. Kaiden says "*Destiny if I said anything to make you sad, I'm sorry.*" Destiny says, "*you're not making me sad I'm fine.*" In the library, Maxwell and Naomi were making out against the bookshelves as Naomi says, "*just because we are doing this doesn't mean I have forgiven you.*" Maxwell lifts her leg as he arches her neck and kisses it. Naomi moans his name as Maxwell says, "*I told you I will prove my love for you.*" As Naomi pulls Maxwell closer, they soon hear voices coming outside as the secretary says, "*why has someone locked the door?*". The caretaker arrives with a key whilst Naomi and Maxwell grab their clothes and come into another room and lock it. The librarian looks inside as the students come in and begin to study. Back in the room, Naomi puts her dress on, and Maxwell does his shirt; The principal comes to the room as Naomi says, "*we are going to get caught.*" Maxwell pulls Naomi under the table as the principal opens the door. Naomi and Maxwell hide under the table as the principal says, " *I don't know what is happening lately with all these door locks.*" As everyone leaves Naomi sighs as Maxwell says, "*that was dangerous sexy doll.*" Naomi gets up and soon leaves whilst Maxwell leaves too after a few minutes.

As Maxwell walks down the corridor, he sees Destiny who comes over to him and says, "*let's do something tonight.*" Maxwell says, "*I am busy, but I will call you.*" Maxwell leaves as Destiny feels he is being distant. Jen comes to Destiny, cheers her up, and says, " *we have practiced this evening.*" Later that afternoon, Kaiden was training the soccer team whilst Destiny and Jen had cheerleading practice. Meanwhile, Naomi got herself dressed in the cheerleading outfit and was about to head out when an arm pulled her into a room. Maxwell says, *"sexy doll you look stunning."* Naomi says, *"Maxwell you have to stop pulling me like this."* Maxwell kisses Naomi and makes out with her. Kaiden heads inside to get some equipment as he hears voices; he passes by the room and is shocked when he sees Naomi and Maxwell kissing through the glass door. Kaiden turns back as he says, *'I can't believe Maxwell would cheat on Destiny.'* Kaiden runs back to the field as Luke says, *"Captain where were you?".* Kaiden says, *"Luke continues with practice; I will be back in two sec."* Kaiden brings Destiny outside to the corridor; as she asks, *"Kaiden why have you brought me here?".* Kaiden opens the door and Destiny looks inside to see it was empty. Kaiden says *"Destiny you need to hear me out; Maxwell was here, and he was with Naomi."* Destiny laughs and says, *"Kaiden are you feeling, ok? Maxwell wouldn't cheat on me."* Kaiden says, *"Destiny please believe me."*

Destiny coldly heads back to practice and says, *"Jen you manage things. I have to go."* Destiny called Maxwell who answered he says, *"babes are you ok?".* Destiny says, *"we need to meet."* He changes and comes to meet Destiny at the college entrance; Destiny asks, *"Maxwell are you cheating on me?".* Maxwell laughs replying, *"babes how can you say that? I love you."* Maxwell hugs Destiny and thinks, *'it's good that me and Naomi left the room when Kaiden saw us.'* Destiny says, *"I don't know what Kaiden was saying; I knew that you would never hurt me."* Later that evening, Kaiden came to speak with Destiny. She says *"Kaiden whatever you saw or think you saw it wasn't real. I spoke with Maxwell, and everything is cleared".* Kaiden says, *"Destiny you must be blind not to see people real's faces."* Destiny was shocked by Kaiden's words, pushes him out and locks the door as he tries to explain. Destiny came to her room and didn't know why but she cried. The next few days went by as Destiny kept her distance from Kaiden. Jen noticed that something was going on with Kaiden and Destiny. Kaiden tells Jen what he saw a few days ago as Jen says, *"Kaiden we need to find some proof and I think you apologise and make it up to Destiny."*

Chapter 33

The weekend finally arrived as Destiny was doing some shopping with Jen however, she couldn't stop talking about Kaiden. Jen says, "*Destiny I know you are mad with Kaiden, but he is our friend.*" Destiny says, "*I know but I wish he wouldn't have lied about Maxwell cheating on me*". Jen tries to explain things however Destiny says, "*not you too.*" Destiny comes home and is surprised to see the place has been decorated. Isabelle says, "*sweetie go and change*". Destiny heads upstairs and has a shower before wearing a flower short dress. As she comes downstairs, she sees Kaiden with his parents as he smiles at her. Destiny angrily asks, "*what are you doing here?*". Kaiden gives her the bouquet of flowers as Destiny throws it on the floor and says, "*just go away.*" She runs upstairs; Isabelle says, "*I am so sorry about my daughter's behaviour.*" Isabelle comes upstairs to Destiny's room and opens to find Destiny's window opened thinking, '*I should give her some space*'. She soon comes back downstairs, Kaiden looks at the photos in the living room as he thinks ' *these photos of Destiny, could it be she is the girl from my childhood?*'. Isabelle says, "*please come and eat.*" Kaiden sneaks upstairs to Destiny's room, looks around and sees the window opened. He looks out to see Destiny sitting on the roof. Kaiden sighs as he climbs out and just as he is about to reach Destiny, he loses his footing.

Destiny sees Kaiden and holds his hand to help him up. Kaiden says "*thanks.*" Destiny asks, "*what are you doing here?*". Kaiden replies, "*I am here to apologise Destiny, I never meant to hurt you.*" Destiny shivers a little as Kaiden takes off his jacket and gives it to her as they look into each other's eyes. Destiny thinks, '*I know this is wrong but why does it feel so right?'*. Kaiden says, *"we'd better get in; I don't know about you, but I am starving."* Destiny laughs as she gets in first. Just then a shooting star passes and Kaiden makes a wish. Destiny helps him get in as they head downstairs; Destiny apologises for earlier. Marie hugs Destiny and says, *"it's ok dear, now come and join us."* Kaiden and Destiny smile as they dig into the feast. Monday morning, Naomi is with Maxwell in the closet making out as Mrs Rosewell opens the door and angrily says *"what is going on in here? get out of me supplies"*. Naomi and Maxwell come out and laughing; Maxwell says, *"sexy doll I love you."* Destiny comes down the corridor as Naomi turns in the opposite direction; Destiny asks, *"Maxwell where were you this weekend?"*. Maxwell rolls his eyes and leaves whilst Destiny wonders, *'what is up with Maxwell?'*.

Jen meets with Destiny who asks, *"did you and Kaiden sort things out?"*. Destiny nods as Destiny say, *"I'll see you in class."* Jen calls Kaiden to meet up outside in a secret spot; Jen says, *"we need to put the plan into action and get the proof."* Kaiden says, *"I don't know about this Jen; won't we be hurting Destiny?"*. Jen says, *"Destiny deserves better Kaiden."* As Kaiden came into class and sat beside Destiny, he asks, *"hey are you excited for the camping trip this weekend?"*. Destiny nods as the teacher comes in and the lesson begins. Jen becomes a spy and sneaks around the corridor and tries to find Naomi and Maxwell. Kaiden is with Destiny at the canteen who wonders, *'where's Jen?'*. Jen texts Kaiden as Kaiden reads the message *'had no luck on finding the cheater'*. Kaiden texts her, *'Destiny is looking for you come soon.'* The next few days pass as Naomi and Maxwell come to meet the coach and speaks with them about the camping trip. Naomi pleads, *"sir I just want another chance. No drama I promise."* Maxwell nods as the coach thinks for a moment and then says, *"ok I will inform Kaiden, Destiny and Jen"*. Later that afternoon, Naomi got changed and came to cheerleading practise whilst Maxwell came to soccer practise. Jen and Kaiden wondered *'what is going on?'*. The coach welcomed back Naomi and Maxwell both in their respected teams' As Jen and Kaiden took a moment to speak alone; Jen says, " *this could be the perfect opportunity to get the proof*".

Chapter 34

J en and Kaiden come back to the field, Destiny asks, "*Jen where did you go?*". Jen replies, "*just a quick break.*" Naomi comes over to the cheerleading squad and gives Destiny a smirk she says, "*I don't want any drama, Naomi.*" Naomi rolls her eyes and sarcastically says, "*sure thing Captain.*" Elsewhere, Maxwell is training with the players as Kaiden watches and gives them tip, Maxwell comes to Kaiden and says, "*I have been captaining for so many years and I know what I am doing.*" Kaiden says "*I want the team to be successful especially for next week's game.*" After the practice, Kaiden, and Jen leave early as Destiny wonders, '*why do I feel like Kaiden, and Jen are hiding something from me?'*. Later that evening Destiny comes to the church, prays, and talks about her feelings when Richelle comes in front of her. Destiny asks, "*who are you? why do you keep appearing in my dreams?*". Richelle replies, "*time is short, and I have already introduced myself, but you will find your happiness soon.*" Richelle speaks in riddles which leaves Destiny feeling confused as someone enters the church and Richelle disappears. Destiny heads home and calls Maxwell who ignores her call as he is with Naomi. Meanwhile, at a restaurant Maxwell asks, "*sexy doll would you like to dance?*" Naomi takes his hand and dance to a sexy tango as he lifts her and spins her. Naomi and Maxwell feel their fire and passion rising between them. Soon, Maxwell pays the bill and takes Naomi home as he opens the door and they pounce on each other hungrily and kissing wildly whilst ripping their clothes off, Naomi says, "*take me to bed.*" Maxwell says, "*your wish is my command sexy doll.*"

The next day at college Destiny tries to look for Maxwell. Meanwhile, Jen and Kaiden are hiding as Mrs. Rosewell spots them. Kaiden says, *"Mrs. Rosewell what a pleasant surprise!"*. Mrs. Rosewell asks, *"what are you two kids up to ere? Not like the two people doing ze nasty in me supplies room."* Jen and Kaiden reply, *"we are not a couple, but you mentioned two people."* Mrs. Rosewell says, *"ze girl Nomi and Max"*. Kaiden and Jen look at each other as Mrs. Rosewell heads to clean up the corridor. Kaiden gives Jen an earpiece and says, *"you can hear me on this right?"*. Jen says, *"I am right next to you silly."* Kaiden whispers something as Jen heads to the right side of the corridor whilst Kaiden takes the left side. Jen walks down, she soon spots Destiny as she is about to turn. Destiny says, *"Jen there you are."* Jen turns asking, *"hey Destiny what are you doing in college so early?"*. Destiny says *" do you have a moment? I need to talk about something."* Jen says, *"of course bestie."* Meanwhile, Kaiden walks down the corridor and looks around he soon hears voices from the stationery photocopier room. Kaiden sees that the glass a black paper blocking it as Kaiden thinks, *'how will I be able to film when there is black paper?'*. He then sees the secretary coming down holding papers; Kaiden comes and says, *"you look like you need a hand Madam."* She smiles and gives Kaiden the paper and comes to the room. she tries to open the door as Maxwell and Naomi see the door handle rattling and head into the cupboard. Kaiden opens the door and removes the black paper as the sectary says, *"every day it's like coming into this room with so much difficulty."* Kaiden looks around and spots a camera thinking, *'I think we have the perfect footage.'*

Elsewhere, Destiny was talking with Jen about Maxwell and everything as Jen says, *"Destiny I feel a little parched can you get me some juice?"*. Kaiden comes out of the room and says to Jen through the earpiece, *"I think I have found a way to get the best footage."* Destiny comes back and gives Jen some juice she says, *"thanks bestie."* Naomi and Maxwell soon come out of the room. Naomi says, *"it's too risky here, we could get caught."* Maxwell holds her by her waist and looks around to the empty corridor and whispers, *"I could take you right here if I wanted but I respect your wishes sexy doll."* Naomi kisses Maxwell and says, *"we can continue our fun at the camping trip."* In class, Maxwell comes to Destiny who says, *"you were acting so weird yesterday."* Maxwell apologies and asks, *"how about we get some dinner tonight?"*. Destiny nods as the teacher comes in and starts the lesson as the day goes by quickly. Jen and Kaiden stay late after college to sneak into the CCTV room, Maxwell takes Destiny on a date and charms her with a ring. Kaiden is able to get the footage and more as Jen and Kaiden leave, they both congratulate each other as they put their plan in motion for the camping trip.

Chapter 35

The next few days pass quickly as the weekend arrives; Kaiden and Jen prepare the plan in secret. Kaiden says, "*Jen this is going to break Destiny.*" Jen says, "*I always knew that Maxwell was a scum but cheating on my best friend he deserves to be humiliated.*" As everyone was on the bus, Maxwell sat with Destiny leaving Naomi feeling jealous however Maxwell text Naomi, '*sexy doll you have nothing to be jealous of, I have a plan for today*'. Soon they reached the campsite near the lake, and everyone unpacked and sat by the fire. The coach says, "*so today we will talk about teamwork.*" The coach sets up a small video as everyone watches and listens when Jen gives Kaiden the signal before they can do anything. Maxwell throws a powder into the fire as it grows stronger creating a small fog; everyone gets back for a moment. Maxwell takes Naomi's hand and heads into the woods. Jen adds her memory card into the machine whilst the coach says, "*I don't know why anyone would do this, especially this powder but if I find out who is responsible then!*". Kaiden says, "*coach I think it was Maxwell.*" Meanwhile, in the woods, Maxwell had Naomi pinned against the tree as Naomi says, "*you naughty boy!*". Maxwell winks and says, "*maybe you should punish me sexy doll!*". Back at the camp, the coach looks around for Maxwell he says, "*I will deal with him later.*"

The coach resumes the video but is left shocked by the next footage as Jen says, "*Destiny I think you should see this.*" Destiny sees Maxwell and Naomi kissing and making out in the photocopier room and parts of the college and is shocked. She gets up and smashes the projector as the cheerleading squad comes around her asking if she is ok. The coach says, *"Destiny, I don't know how that recording got on."* Destiny asks, *"did you know about them?"*. The coach shakes his head as everyone says, *"we are just as shocked as you are"*. Just then, Maxwell and Naomi came back and wondered what was going on; Destiny asks, *"Maxwell did you have a nice time?."* Maxwell pretends to play innocent as Destiny grabs him and pushes him into the lake. Maxwell gets up soaked as he says angrily, *"Destiny what the hell!"*. Destiny removes the ring and says *"you are cheating lying scumbag, don't you ever talk to me ever! WE ARE DONE!"*. Destiny comes into her tent as the coach says, *"you and Naomi are to leave immediately!"*. Naomi helps Maxwell out of the water as Jen pushes her in and says, *"you both deserve this!"*. Naomi and Maxwell grab their stuff and leave. Jen tries to console Destiny. The coach says, *"if you all want to go home."* Kaiden says, *"no coach we still have one more day and despite what has happened we are a team."* As Monday approaches Destiny comes to the coach's office to hand her in the notice and says, *"I am no longer able to be captain, please can all my responsibilities be given to Jen."* The coach tries to talk her out of it however she leaves the room. Destiny comes to class as Naomi mocks her saying, *"Maxwell wanted a real person and that's me and you are nothing but a play toy."* Destiny grabs her bag and eaves the class. Maxwell comes in and Naomi says, *"Maxy we no longer need to hide our relationship."*

Maxwell feels guilty as Destiny is heartbroken. she cries outside and is not able to focus on her studies. Maxwell wants to explain things to Destiny however she pushes him aside and says, *"I told you I don't ever want to talk to you."* Maxwell says, *"is it any wonder that someone like you is cheated on! you can't even give me what I want, and I have Naomi now."* Destiny slaps Maxwell as he pushes her aside. Naomi comes to Maxwell as Destiny runs out of the college. Jen and Kaiden hear what has happened. Kaiden punches Maxwell and says, *"someone like you never deserved Destiny."* At home, Destiny is still in pain as Isabelle notices and asks, *"sweetie are you ok?"*. Destiny heads to her room and is lost in thoughts when she gets a call from Jen but doesn't answer. Kaiden calls Destiny however Destiny doesn't pick up either. Destiny opens her drawer to the locket that Maxwell gave her, she heads out and comes to Maxwell's place. Naomi opens the door in Maxwell's shirt as Naomi rolls her eyes and says, "*why have you come here?*". Destiny throws the locket at Maxwell and leaves. She passes the church and comes in; she cries and breaks down as Richelle comes in front of her. Destiny says, "*you are here to laugh at my pain, right?*". Destiny continues, "*you told me that I would find happiness, but you never said my heart will be broken.*" Richelle says, "*your heart will heal, and you will find true love, but I cannot say more than this.*" As Richelle disappears Destiny falls to the ground shouting, "*WHY ME? WHY DID YOU HAVE TO HURT ME SO MUCH?*". Destiny runs home, locks her room as Kaiden and Jen meet; they both are worried for her. Jen says, "*coach told me that Destiny has left the cheerleading squad*". Kaiden says, "*let me try to talk to her.*" Later that evening, Kaiden climbs the pipe and knocks on Destiny's window. Destiny opens her window as Kaiden is about to fall as Destiny holds his hand and pulls him in; he falls on top of her and their lips kiss.

Chapter 36

Destiny gets up and helps Kaiden who looks at her and apologizes. He says, *"it's late and I didn't want to disturb your parents."* Destiny sighs and asks, *"Kaiden what are you doing here?".* Kaiden says, *"we need to talk."* Kaiden sees Destiny is sad and says, *"I know you are still hurting after seeing Maxwell's betrayal."* Destiny says, *"I am not mad just sad about it and whoever is responsible for doing that."* Kaiden looks nervous as Destiny senses that Kaiden is hiding something as she says *" Kaiden look at me."* Kaiden looks at Destiny as he says, *"I am sorry, but I and Jen were the one who found out Maxwell's secret and took the footage."* Destiny felt angry and says, *"how could you two do this to me? you're supposed to be my friends."* Destiny opens the window and pushes Kaiden before he can explain. He lands on the grass as Destiny says, *"I hate you both."* The next morning, Destiny comes to college, Jen sees her and says, *"hey Destiny."* Destiny looks at Jen coldly who comes over and asks, *" is everything ok? did Kaiden explain everything?".* Destiny laughs and replies, *"what's there to explain? My best friends stabbed me in the back."* A small crowd gathers around them as Jen says, *"Destiny what are you saying?".* Destiny cries as she says, *"you and Kaiden playing the video in front of everyone, did you even think how I would have felt for a second?".* Jen says, *"you have no right to be mad at me or Kaiden, we tried to warn you."* Destiny says, *"what hurts more is that we have been friends since kids, and you've hurt me in the worst possible way."*

Destiny turns and runs as Kaiden comes down the corridor to Jen. Everyone soon walks away whilst Jen turns to Kaiden asking, *"what did you say to Destiny? how could you tell her that we were the one who exposed Maxwell? you didn't fully explain everything?".* Kaiden sighs *"I never got the chance to, she flung me out of the window."* Jen sighs, they both come to class as Destiny in the corner and doesn't look at Kaiden or Jen. The teacher comes in and says, *"everyone I hope you have been working hard for the end-of-year exam in a few weeks."* Kitty and Michelle looked around and wondered *' where's Naomi?'.* Elsewhere, Naomi was in the bathroom as she was vomiting and felt ill. Kitty texted Naomi who soon replied *'bath'* and collapsed. Kitty saw Naomi's text and showed Michelle; Michelle says, *"Naomi must be in the bathroom."* After class finishes, they both run to the bathroom to find Naomi on the floor unconscious. Kitty says, *"someone call an ambulance."* As the ambulance comes and takes Naomi, Maxwell looks at Kitty asking, *"what's going on?".* Kitty replies, *"Maxwell you need to go with Naomi."* Before the ambulance can close their door; Maxwell says, *"I am Naomi's boyfriend."* Maxwell comes in and holds Naomi's hand and kisses it and says, *"sexy doll you will be ok."*

At college Destiny is in the canteen as she thinks about everything, she wonders *' was I hard on Jen and Kaiden?'.* She decides to make things right and calls Jen who comes and says, *"Destiny if you called me to have another go, don't bother."* Destiny says, *"I ordered your favourite milkshake."* Destiny sighs and says, *"I am sorry for having a go at you earlier, I know you would never intentionally hurt me."* Jen says *" of course I wouldn't, how could you think that? Maxwell is a cheating scumbag, and you deserve better!".* Destiny hugs Jen who says, *"there's someone else you need to sort things out with."* Destiny nods as Kaiden was out of college. He made a call to arrange a special surprise for Destiny. At the hospital Naomi soon gain conscious and looked around to see Maxwell beside her. Naomi asks, *"Maxy where am I?",* the doctor comes in with Naomi's results and says, *"congratulation you are pregnant."* Naomi and Maxwell were both stunned as the doctor says, *"I will advise rest and also some medicines."* Naomi smiled saying, *"Maxy we are going to be parents."* Maxwell headed out whilst Naomi looked sadly wondering, *'is Maxwell going to abandon me and the baby?'.*

Chapter 37

After college, Destiny looks for Kaiden and wonders *'where is he?'*. She calls his mobile however it goes to voicemail; as Jen comes to Destiny and asks, *"have you spoken to Kaiden?"*. Destiny shakes her head and says, *"I haven't found him yet and he isn't answering his phone."* Jen gets a call from her mom and says, *"I need to go."* Destiny walks down her street, sees Kaiden's house and goes over. She rings the bell as Marie opens and says, *"Destiny sweetie what a nice surprise."* Destiny asks, *"is Kaiden home?"*. Marie replies, *"no sweetie."* Destiny leaves a message as she heads back to her house. Marie closes the door as she says, *"Kaiden, Destiny came to see you and you made me lie that you are not in."* Kaiden says, *"she pushed me out of a window mom."* Marie sighs and says, *"you two should really sort things out."* Meanwhile back in the hospital, Kitty and Michelle came to visit Naomi; they brought balloons and food. Naomi says, *"you girls are the best."* Kitty asks, *"we were so worried."* Michelle asks, *"is everything ok?"*. Naomi takes a deep breath, sits up and says, *"I am pregnant."* They are both surprised and have lots of questions to ask when the door opens and Maxwell says, *"can you give me two minutes please girls?"*.

Kitty and Michelle leave as Naomi says, *"Maxy, I know you must be scared and if you don't want anything to do with the baby."* Maxwell kisses her and says, *"sexy doll I was so surprised, but you are giving our love a symbol."* Naomi felt worried however Maxwell took her hand and kissed it assuring her, *"you and I will be the best parents."* Maxwell gives Naomi a small teddy. She smiles and embraces Maxwell happily. Elsewhere, Kaiden calls Jen to meet in the desert parlour; Jen asks, *"Kaiden did you speak with Destiny?".* Kaiden shakes his head as she continues, *"Destiny was looking for you."* Kaiden seemed surprised look at Jen whilst she explained how they sorted the misunderstandings. Kaiden thought for a moment and looked at his phone, *'should I call Destiny?'.* However, he put his phone in his pocket and says, *"don't worry Jen I have something special planned for tomorrow."* Jen says, *"you love Destiny, don't you?".* Kaiden looked at Jen who says, *"you two should get together, you are a better choice than Maxwell."* It soon gets late, Kaiden comes home and looks across the street at Destiny's house thinking, *'I hope tomorrow I will be able to tell you everything.'*

Meanwhile, Destiny was in her room, she couldn't help but think of Kaiden and thought, *'is he mad at me for throwing him out the window? could it be he hates me?'.* Destiny didn't know why she felt upset and cried over Kaiden. The next morning at college, Kaiden ignored Destiny when she approached him. Jen notices and comes over to Destiny who is hurt. Destiny says, *"he hates me that why he doesn't want to listen to me."* Destiny headed to the library whilst Jen came to class and sat beside Kaiden. She says, *"I didn't know your plan was to hurt Destiny."* Kaiden was stunned and says, *"I would never hurt her."* Jen says, *"she thinks you hate her."* Kaiden sighs and says, *"I will go speak with her."* Destiny came into the library and thought, *'I am not going to think about Kaiden.'* Kaiden came up behind her and blindfolded her. He lifts her in his arms as Destiny says, *"who are you? where are you taking me?".* Kaiden's first stop is at a small café, he feeds Destiny her favourite cake as she says, *"this is yummy."* She tries to take off her blindfold; Kaiden kisses her and says, *"if you take your blindfold off before this evening, I will keep kissing you."* Destiny blushes hearing Kaiden's words. He brings her shopping and buys her a new outfit before finally bringing her to his final surprise. Destiny asks, *"can I remove my blindfold now?".* Kaiden replies, *"of course.".* Destiny unfolds the blindfold and looks around, she smiles and says, *"wow this is amazing."* Kaiden hands her an outfit as Destiny takes it and heads to the changing room. Kaiden watches her leaving smiling. Destiny changes into the outfit and looks in the mirror and thinks, *'wow Kaiden is so sweet.'*

Chapter 38

Destiny comes out and looks for Kaiden, Kaiden puts some music on and holds a rope as he says, *"Destiny take my hand."* Kaiden sings, *"You know I need you, I'm not trying to hide it*

I know you need me, So don't keep pushing me away, You claim it's just a fling, But I don't see that, And I try to reach out to you, But your in my heart, So don't stop me, so are you and I meant to be? So why don't we rewrite the stars? Say you were meant to be with me, nothing will keep us apart, you'd be the one I was meant to find, it's up to you and it's up to me, No one can pull us apart, so why don't we rewrite our story? Maybe we'll be together, tonight". Destiny takes Kaiden's hand as she sings, *"You think like me, You think I want you , But there are obstacles in our way, And there are doors that are locked, I know you're wondering why we're not able to be, just us With these walls in the way*

we are kept apart, You're gonna see, it's hopeless for us, No, we can't rewrite the stars

How can you say that we're meant to be, Everything keeps pulling us apart, And I'm not the one for you, It's not up to you, It's not up to me, When everyone tells us to keep moving on

How can we rewrite our story?, Maybe we can't be together, Tonight". Destiny drops to the floor and searches for Kaiden who swings and grabs Destiny as they sing together. *"all I want is to be with you, all I want is to see you everyday, so just give me a chance"*. Destiny sings, *" it feels impossible"*. Kaiden sings, *"it's possible, I see"*. They sing together, *"let's rewrite the stars?, Say we're meant to be, nothing will keep us apart, cause you're with me*

It's up to you and it's up to me, no one can change our mind let's rewrite the stars". Kaiden spins Destiny as she does acrobatics tricks and twirls with Kaiden singing, *"You know I like you, It's like I don't need to hide it, but we are not meant to be, the walls will break, everything will keep us apart, tonight"*. They both stop as Kaiden holds her close as they feel each other's heartbeat. Kaiden says, *"Destiny, I have something to tell you"*. Destiny looks at him and says, *"tell me, Kaiden"*. Kaiden confesses his feelings as Destiny kisses him passionately. He holds her and strokes her face lovingly; Destiny says, *" I have feelings for you too Kaiden"*. They look at each other as Kaiden says, *"I know you've recently broken up with Maxwell, but I will wait for you"*. Destiny smiles at Kaiden who goes over and turns off the music. Destiny heads to change as does Kaiden. Later that evening Destiny heads to the church, prays, and thinks about her wonderful day with Kaiden. Destiny lights a candle and wonders, *'am I ready to be in another relationship? am I falling deep in Kaiden's love?'*. Kaiden comes home and thinks of Destiny, *'I hope she will give me a chance?'*. Destiny showers and logs onto her laptop as she sees a star shower tomorrow evening and thinks, *'this will be the perfect opportunity to confess my love to him.'* The next day at college, Destiny is with Jen who asks, *"where did you disappear to yesterday?"*. Destiny doesn't say anything but blushes when Kaiden passes her.

Jen notices this asking, *"Destiny do you like Kaiden?"*. Destiny nudges Jen and says, *"do you have to make it obvious?"*. Soon, Destiny avoids Kaiden in class, he looks sad wondering, *'is Destiny mad at me that she doesn't want to talk or sit with me?'*. At break Destiny brings Jen to the park and says, *"I have a plan for tonight."* Destiny gets a queue barrier around the tree whilst Jen asks, *"what are you planning to do?"*. Destiny tells Jen about the star shower as Jen says, *"I am so happy for you."* They head back to college, Destiny heads to class whilst Jen comes to her locker to get some books. She turns and walks down however ends up bumping into someone knocking all her books out of her arm.

Jen annoyed says, *"can't you see where you are going numbnuts?"*. Jen looks at the person with green eyes, she thinks, *'wow he has sparkly emerald eyes.'* Luke apologizes and says, *"I am sorry Jen."* The bell rings for class; Luke stops Jen asking, *"Jen would you like to hang out after school?"*. Jen replies, *"Aww are you asking me on a date?"*. Luke is nervous whilst Jen smiles and says, *"sure how about we go cinema?"*. Luke nods as he says, *"well we'd better get to class."* Jen and Luke share a smile at each other, Destiny notices asking, *"Jen are you hiding something?."* At lunch Kaiden comes over to Destiny and Jen. Destiny says, *"I have something to work on."* Kaiden sighs as he says to Jen, *"I thought we had a moment yesterday."* Jen sees Luke who comes over to her, as Kaiden says *"hey Luke what's up?"*. Luke asks, *"is this seat available?"*. Jen replies, *"you can sit here."* Kaiden gives Luke and Jen some privacy and finishes his lunch.

At the hospital Naomi is finally able to leave as Maxwell helps her. They head home Maxwell says, *"Naomi, I think you should take some leave from college."* Naomi says, *"Maxy I am fine, and I can't wait to get back."* They both argue as Maxwell storms out and Naomi throws a cushion at the door. As nightfall approaches Destiny brings Kaiden to the park blindfolded as he says, *"let me guess you have a special surprise for me."* Destiny lays a small blanket on the floor and says, *"you can look now."* Kaiden removes his blindfold and sees Destiny who she points to the sky where there are billions of stars it begins to rain like shooting stars. Kaiden says *"wow it's so beautiful."* Destiny comes closer to Kaiden and kisses him; he holds her close. Kaiden breaks the kiss and says, *"Destiny I thought you didn't feel the same."* Destiny replies, *"I love you Kaiden and I want us to be together."* They both sit on the blanket and watch the stars twinkle in the sky, they get closer and share another kiss as Kaiden places her head on Destiny's lap and says, *"being here with you feels so warm and lovely."* Destiny feels happiness as she plays with Kaiden's hair. Meanwhile at the cinema, Jen and Luke are having a great time watching, *'Spiderman No way home'.* Luke reaches for the popcorn and touches Jen's hand; he apologizes as Jen turns and comes closer and kisses Luke who is surprised. Jen says, *"Luke just kiss me."* Luke does this and thinks, *'wow her lips are so soft like strawberries, I have never felt this way about any girl before.'* Luke breaks the kiss as the movie ends, Jen takes his hand and says, *"I want to give our relationship a chance."* Luke smiles and leaves with Jen happily; The next few weeks pass by at college as Naomi and Maxwell seem to be fighting a lot. Naomi tries to keep her pregnancy hidden however Destiny and Jen find out when they see Naomi in the bathroom. Naomi asks, *"what do you want to rub it in my face?".* Jen rolls her eyes whilst Destiny says, *"look I know we have had our differences, but I have moved on."* Naomi and Destiny manage to sort things out as Maxwell overhears Destiny mention Kaiden. Maxwell thinks, *'I can't believe geek-boy took my girl'.* Later that afternoon, Naomi is in the mall doing baby shopping and tries to call Maxwell but no answer.

Chapter 39

In the evening Kaiden and Destiny came home holding hands. Destiny says, *"I love you Kaiden."* Kaiden pulls her closer and they share a kiss as he replies, *"I love you more."* Maxwell claps and comes over as he says, *"you deserve an award Destiny Miller."* Kaiden asks, *"Maxwell what are you doing here?"*. Maxwell rolls his eyes and replies, *"none of your business."* Maxwell says, *"we were together for so many years and you never gave me the one thing I wanted."* Destiny looks at him coldly and says, *"for you, a relationship needs to be based on sex right!?."* Maxwell says, *"I have my sexy doll to satisfy my needs."* Destiny felt disgusted whilst Kaiden says, *"leave Maxwell."* Maxwell says, *"you can try to tame the virgin queen and get her to give it out especially since you are second trash."* Kaiden grabs his collar as Maxwell laughs coldly. Destiny says, *"Kaiden leave him he's not worth it."* Kaiden says, *"he doesn't get to disrespect you like this."* Kaiden lets go of Maxwell's collar as he gets up and walks into the road and insults Destiny more. An incoming car drives and hits him. Destiny screams, *"MAXWELL!"*. Maxwell rolls over the car and lands on the road cover in blood. Kaiden and Destiny come over as the driver calls an ambulance. Kaiden says, *"Destiny, step back"*. Kaiden bends down to Maxwell who feels his eyes closing and holds his hand saying, *"Maxwell you need to get better for Naomi."* Maxwell looks at Destiny and Kaiden as he says *" I...m...sor...rry."* His hand drops from Kaiden, Destiny closes her eyes shocked with tears running down as Kaiden closes Maxwell's eyes. He sees Maxwell's broken phone. Naomi calls Maxwell: Kaiden answers and says, *"Naomi we need to talk."* Naomi gets worried asking, *"what happened? Why are*

you answering Maxy's phone?". Kaiden holds Destiny who replies, *"Maxwell is dead."* Naomi screams as Kitty and Michelle are beside her and Naomi drops the phone in shock. Kitty takes the phone and speaks to Kaiden who tells her about Maxwell's death.

Soon, the ambulance arrives and takes Maxwell's body, the car driver says, *"I tried to stop but he came right in front of my car."* Kaiden assures him that it was a tragic accident. Kaiden sits with Destiny who says, *"it still doesn't feel real, Maxwell's death."* Kaiden holds Destiny's hand and comforts her. The next day at college everyone finds out about Maxwell's death whilst Naomi plans the funeral for him. Kitty and Michelle help as Destiny, Jen, Luke, Kaiden, and everyone pay their respect. Destiny places a white tulip on his grave as Naomi places a red rose and says, *"rest in peace my love."* A few days pass, as the college decides to hold a small memorial for Maxwell. Destiny says a few words about Maxwell as Naomi soon gets on stage and pours her heart out before saying, *"I have decided to leave college."* Kitty and Michelle were stunned as Naomi runs out of the room. Destiny comes out to see Naomi crying and says, *"Maxwell was taken from me, and I don't think I can be here as everything reminds me of him."* Destiny says, *"you have your child Naomi, you are not alone."* Naomi says, *"thanks Destiny".* Kaiden comes to Destiny and asks, *"are you ok?".* Destiny replies, *"I will be fine."*

Time flies by as final exams arrive as Destiny, Jen, Kaiden, Luke, and everyone takes the exam to prepare them for the future. They finish the exam and head out; Luke says, *"I think we should all go out for a milkshake."* Jen kisses Luke and says, *"sounds cool!".* Destiny and Kaiden join them for a milkshake as Jen says, *"it feels like we are on a double-date."* Destiny smiles and shares a milkshake with Kaiden. Jen says, *"you two are so adorable."* Luke feeds Jen a cherry and kisses her cheek and says, *"you're the cutest."* Kaiden and Destiny leave Jen and Luke to romance and head out together. Destiny and Kaiden hang out at the park under the tree; Kaiden says, *"sometimes I wish time would stop."* Destiny says, *"we can't control time, but we can live in the moments."*

They share a kiss as Destiny's phone rings. Jen says, "*Destiny I can't believe you left me and Luke to go romance, I needed to speak with you about prom.*" Destiny says, "*Kaiden I need to go.*" Kaiden asks, "*can I drop you home?*". Destiny shakes her head and leaves. Kaiden sits under the tree as he gets a call from Luke regarding prom, Kaiden says "*that must be why the girls left us.*" Kaiden and Luke plan a special surprise for their girls. Jen comes to meet Destiny who says, "*we need to get new outfits.*" Destiny says, "*hold on Jen, the guys haven't asked us yet.*" Jen sighs and says, "*you're right.*" The next day at college early morning Jen gets taken to the field as Luke prepares a special surprise and assembles the soccer team to hold signs. Jen reads it, '*WILL YOU BE MY DATE TO PROM JEN?*'. Luke kicks a ball that explodes with glitter and sprinkles over Jen; she nods and runs into his arm as he lifts and kisses her happily. Destiny watches Jen and Luke and thinks, '*wow she is so lucky to have him.*' Destiny comes inside and sees a path of red rose petals. She walks down the corridor as it gets dark, but candles illuminate the path; Destiny sees Kaiden in a heart of candles on his knees holding a box as the lights come back on.

Chapter 40

Kaiden says, "*Destiny you are the love of my life, would you do me the honours of being my prom date?*". He opens the box to reveal a ring; Destiny nods and runs to him with tears in her eyes. He puts the ring on her finger and lifts her as she kisses him passionately. Destiny sees a heart balloon on top of her, she pops it, and confetti pours on her and Kaiden, Everyone around them cheers for them. Jen and Luke come in as Luke says, "*well-done bro!*". Jen pulls Destiny as she says, "*I guess that means we are getting new outfits.*" Jen takes Destiny shopping; they go to many shops before Jen finally manages to get a beautiful long blue dress, Destiny finds a purple lilac party dress; the girls pamper themselves as Kaiden and Luke get dressed and get their girls a corsage. Kaiden arranges a limo as Destiny says, "*Kaiden is such a sweetheart.*" Jen says, "*Luke is sweeter than Kaiden.*" Destiny and Jen argue on who is better, they both stop and start laughing. Destiny says, "*I never thought we would have an argument over whose boyfriend is better.*" As the limo approaches Luke and Kaiden come out, as Marie and Isabelle are nearby and says, "*you are not leaving until photos.*" They do various poses as they do individual photos. Marie says, "*my little boy is all grown up.*" Kaiden says, "*mom please.*" Jen, Kaiden, and Luke come into the limo; Destiny looks down the road and sees a white light. She thinks, '*that's strange!*'. Kaiden says, "*come in babes.*" Soon, they reach prom, and everyone is dancing and enjoying the food. Jen says, "*let's start with the food and then dance.*" Luke takes Jen's hand and head in as Kaiden extends his hand to Destiny and says, "*my lady.*" Destiny smiles and takes Kaiden's hand as they dance; the principal comes on stage and says, *"I have a very special announcement to make! First, Welcome to Senior Prom!"*. The students cheer and dance, the principal says, *"I know it's early, but I would like to announce your Prom King and Queen."* As the students wait to see who it is; the principal says, *"Congratulations to Kaiden Turner and Destiny Miller."* Jen yells, *"THAT'S MY BESTIE!"*. They come on stage, the principal gives them each a crown as Destiny and Kaiden make a small toast. They head back to the stage and dance. Kaiden spins Destiny as she feels warmth and love in his arms. Destiny says, *"Kaiden I'm falling in love with you more every minute."* Kaiden says *"I have something to show you."* Kaiden takes Destiny back to his room and shows her a photo of two kids as Destiny says, *"that's me when I was little."* Kaiden says *"yeah little Destiny who always stood by my side."* Kaiden has a tear in his eyes as Destiny comes closer, *"don't cry Kaiden I promise I will never leave your side ever."* Kaiden and Destiny kiss passionately they soon remove their clothes as Kaiden strokes Destiny and says, *"do you want this?"*. Destiny nods and says, *"I want you Kaiden and I have never been surer!"*. As their kiss gets more passionate; Destiny looks at the light which is getting brighter. She gets up as Kaiden asks, *"Destiny are you ok?"*. Destiny looks around as the room begins to disappear into a white background as Kaiden reaches out to Destiny and says, *"Destiny I won't let you leave."* Destiny says, *"Kaiden I love you..."* As a small explosion happens, Destiny opens her eyes to see a space-like surrounding and sees herself in a white dress. Richelle appears in front of her; Destiny says, *"who are you? why have you brought me here?"*. Richelle blows a cloud of small dust in the air; Destiny sees on the screen a past version of her life before the accident. Destiny says, *"I died in the past and Kaiden..."*; Richelle says, *"it's your final choice of what you decide now."*

Destiny thinks about everything and looks at Richelle replying, *"I want to go back to Kaiden I love him, and I can't live without him."* Richelle says, *"I have witnessed your true love and your journey to be with him forever."* Richelle blows another dust at the air; Destiny sees her younger self playing with a little boy and says, *"it's Kaiden, he has always been with me."* Richelle wipes a tear from her eyes as she looks at Destiny and sprinkles dust over Destiny who closes her eyes just before there is another explosion. Two years have passed as Destiny is at a party; she feels her stomach and attends to the guest. A young girl runs to her as Kaiden comes and lifts her and says, *"Dahlia sweetie, you mustn't run so fast.".* Dahlia says, *"I want mommy."* Destiny holds Dahlia as she asks, *"am I getting a sister or brother?".* Destiny smiles and puts Dahlia down as she gathers everyone and says, *"there are two reasons for this party, tell them babes."* Kaiden says *"yes the first is to celebrate our two-year wedding anniversary and of course find out what baby we are having."* The crowd cheers as Kaiden brings the balloon; Destiny lifts Dahlia as she pops it with blue confetti as Dahlia says happily, *"I don't mind having a baby brother."* Kaiden and Destiny share a kiss, Destiny attends to the guest as Luke is holding his son, Destiny comes over asking, *"how is the little football star?".* Luke replies, *"amazing as always, congratulations on your little boy."* Jen comes over with her daughter Sophia. Sophia says, *"Auntie Destiny."* They share a hug; Destiny sees Naomi in the corner with a little boy who resembles Maxwell. She comes over as Naomi says, *"congratulations on your little boy."* Naomi says, *"I can't thank you enough Destiny for helping me in these two years."* Naomi cries Destiny gives her a hug and says, *" you deserve happiness."* Destiny feels tired as Kaiden comes behind her and says, *"I missed my Destiny."* Destiny says, *"I feel so big."* Kaiden says *" you are the most beautiful and gorgeous woman on earth."* They share a kiss as Destiny places Kaiden's hand on her stomach and feels the baby's kicks.

One year later Destiny and Kaiden are celebrating Christmas with their little boy whom they have named Charlie. Dahlia sees the snow outside and says, *"Daddy I want to make a snowman".* Kaiden lifts Dahlia as they head outside to make a snowman; Kaiden says *"snowman can make wishes come true".* Dahlia laughs and says, *"silly daddy".* Kaiden helps Dahlia to add the finishing touches. Dahlia says, *"take my photo please, daddy"*. Kaiden and Dahlia take a selfie by the snowman. Kaiden says, *"Dahlia you still haven't told me your wish sweetie"*. Dahlia looks at Kaiden and says, *"when I grow up, I want to fall in love with a man who loves me as much as you love mommy!"* Kaiden takes Dahlia in his arms and says, *"your wish will come true"*. Soon, it begins to snow heavily, Kaiden brings Dahlia inside. Dahlia plays with her little brother whilst Destiny and Kaiden come outside in the evening. They look at the sky filled with stars as Kaiden holds Destiny close and says, *" I am thankful you came into my life and gave me happiness."* Destiny turns to face Kaiden who says, *"you have shown me the true meaning of love and gave me everything I ever wanted."* They share a kiss as Dahlia says, *"mummy, daddy come inside"*. Destiny and Kaiden head back inside, above the clouds and deep in space Richelle watches Destiny and Kaiden love and smiles happily.